PROMISED GIFTS

A CASTLE MOUNTAIN LODGE ROMANCE

ELENA AITKEN

INK BLOT COMMUNICATIONS

ISBN: 978-1-927968-69-7

ALSO BY ELENA AITKEN

Timber Creek

When We Left

When We Were Us

Castle Mountain Lodge

Unexpected Gifts

Hidden Gifts

Unexpected Endings - Short Story

Mistaken Gifts

Secret Gifts

Goodbye Gifts

Tempting Gifts

Holiday Gifts

Promised Gifts

Accidental Gifts

The Castle Mountain Lodge Complete Collection

The Springs Series

Summer of Change

Falling Into Forever

Winter's Burn

Midnight Springs

Second Glances

She's Making A List

The Seasons: Volume 1

The Seasons: Volume 2

Fighting For Forever

The Springs Complete Collection - Books 1-10

The Springs—Stone Summit

Summit of Desire

Summit of Seduction

Summit of Passion

Stone Summit Trilogy

The McCormicks

Love in the Moment

Going for the Moment

Only for a Moment

One more Moment

In this Moment

From this Moment

Bears of Grizzly Ridge

His to Protect

His to Seduce

His to Claim

Hers to Take

Bears of Grizzly Ridge: The Complete Set

Destination Paradise

Shelter by the Sea

Escape to the Sun

Hidden in the Sand - Available 2019

Escape Collection

Nothing Stays in Vegas

Return to Vegas

Drawing Free

Sugar Crash

Composing Myself

Betty & Veronica

The Escape Collection

Halfway Series

Halfway to Nowhere

Halfway in Between

Halfway to Christmas

PROMISED GIFTS

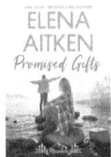

You're invited back to Castle Mountain Lodge!

For as long as she could remember, Marissa Duncan had been completely and totally in love with her older brother's best friend. She spent her teenage years secretly crushing on Nick Slater until one day—sure he felt the same way— she got up the courage to tell him how she felt.

But instead of reciprocating her affection, the boy she'd fallen in love with had laughed in her face and sent her away broken hearted.

It's been five years since Nick has seen Marissa Duncan. Five years that he hasn't been able to stop thinking about her and what could have been if he'd followed his heart the night she'd confessed her love to him. But the timing hadn't been right, and there was a code between friends. He couldn't date his best friends little sister. No matter what.

For five years, Marissa has managed to avoid Nick, but there will be no way to avoid him at her brother's wedding at Castle Mountain Lodge, the most romantic location in the Rockies. Especially since Nick's the best man, and she's agreed to be the maid of honor. She has no reason to be nervous, after all, she's no longer the awkward, uncertain teenager she once was. Besides, what she felt for Nick was only a childhood crush.

Things have changed.

Haven't they?

"Well? It's beautiful, don't you think?"

Marissa Duncan could think of at least a dozen words off the top of her head to describe the poof of lavender fabric she was wearing, but beautiful was *not* one of them.

She looked down at the skirt and attempted to smooth the dress down before she looked up to her sister-in-law to-be's eyes. Jenny looked so anxious, clearly desperate for Marissa to like the dress that she forced a smile and nodded. "It's very...full."

"It is, isn't it? Jake said you really liked the traditional dress styles from the eighties."

"He did not?"

Everything was starting to make sense, and she was going to outright kill her brother when she saw him.

"I mean, it wouldn't have been my first pick." Jenny was still talking. "But Jake said you used to play dress-up in your mom's old gowns and you really liked the fluffy ones."

"He did, did he?" Marissa spun to face the mirror and her poofy, purple self. She shook her head slightly but couldn't help but smile. Her big brother always did like to prank her. It was wishful thinking to assume he'd grown out of it.

Even when it came to his own wedding.

"You like it, don't you?" Jenny looked so hopeful, and Marissa knew she was already under so much stress with her wedding and her own best friend unable to stand up for her, she couldn't bear to upset her even more. After all, Jenny was going to be her sister-in-law, and she was a sweet girl. It was just a dress. She'd live.

"If you're happy, I'm happy." Marissa smiled.

Jenny's face lit up and she impulsively wrapped her arms around Marissa. "Oh, I am," she said. "I'm so happy to be marrying your brother and to have you as my sister." She released her, and swiped at her face.

"Jenny, don't cry. You're happy, remember?"

"I am." She made a sound somewhere between a laugh and a cry that came out much more snort-like than was no doubt intended. "I really am. And I really do want to thank you again for agreeing to be my maid of honor."

"It's my pleasure." While they spoke, Marissa slipped into the changing room to shed herself of the dress. "And I know I'm no replacement for Sara, but I'll do my best."

Jenny's best friend, Sara, had been called away to England suddenly because her grandmother was ill. So, when Jenny asked Marissa if she'd do the honors, there was no way she could refuse.

"You're going to be great," Jenny said through the curtain. "And it feels so right to have you there with Jake and me. I know how close you two are. Things just worked out the way they were supposed to."

She was close with her brother. Only eleven months her senior, they'd grown up spending a lot of time together, and although of course they'd definitely had their moments when they drove each other crazy, Jake was legitimately one of Marissa's closest friends. Despite the purple monstrosity he'd tricked her into wearing. She rolled her eyes one more time at the bridesmaid dress before carefully hanging it up, although she couldn't imagine any scenario where she could possibly crush the poof out of it. Even with her best effort.

Not that there was any time anyway. Right after the fitting, they were leaving for all the pre-wedding activities. The wedding was taking place in only a few days, at the beautiful and utterly romantic Castle Mountain Lodge in the Rockies. It was only a few hours away from the city, and Marissa had only been there one other time, a few years earlier for a girlfriend's birthday weekend. Everything about the Lodge was absolutely perfect for a wedding. When she heard Jake and Jenny were tying the knot there, she was both thrilled for them and jealous at the same time. Not that she was close to getting married herself.

She'd have to at least have a boyfriend for that.

Marissa wiggled into her black jeans and slid the gauzy summer blouse over her head before she slipped out of the changing room and joined Jenny. "When's your family flying in? I haven't even met your brother yet."

Jenny's family lived mostly out East. Although her parents had been in town for the last few weeks, her brother hadn't arrived yet and she was looking forward to meeting him because he was going to be filling in as Jake's best man. It was kind of ironic really, and a bit sad, that both the bride's and the groom's best friends couldn't be at the wedding.

Not that Marissa was upset that Nick Slater, her brother's best friend, wouldn't be there.

Not really.

She hadn't seen Nick in eight years. And she didn't even want to think about how mortifying that last meeting had been.

For years, she'd been so desperately in love with her brother's best friend, until finally, sure that he must feel the same way, she'd taken a chance and kissed him on the night of her graduation dance.

It had been the single best moment of her life.

Until he'd laughed.

Nick Slater had laughed at her.

And broken her heart.

It had been eight years ago, but she still remembered it as if it were yesterday.

Yes, it was definitely better that Nick couldn't make it to the wedding.

Marissa shook her head and focused on the matter at hand. There was no point dwelling on the past. "So, when is the best man showing up?"

"Oh," Jenny looked up from her wedding planning binder and blinked, as if she'd just heard Marissa. "You mean my Josh?"

"He *is* the best man, after all." Marissa got a sinking feeling in the pit of her stomach.

"Oh, no." Jenny shook her head. "I mean, he was going to be because Jake's best friend couldn't make it."

"Nick."

"Right." Jenny smiled. "I forget that you must know him, too. Nick Slater. He wasn't going to be able to make it to the wedding, something about a meeting overseas that he couldn't get out of or something, but he worked some magic and..."

Marissa had stopped listening. Instead, an intense buzzing had filled her head.

Nick. He was going to be there? At the wedding. That they left for in only a few hours.

She shook her head, more in an effort to shake out the noise than anything else, but it didn't work.

"Marissa?" Jenny's hand pressed to her arm. "Are you okay? Do you need some air or some water?"

Marissa managed a nod. "I'm fine." There was no way Jenny could have known that Nick meant anything more to her than just being her brother's best friend.

Not unless Nick had said something to Jake about the kiss. But he hadn't. She would have known, because Jake would have teased her relentlessly because of it.

No. He hadn't told.

But she knew.

For eight years, she'd managed to avoid him. But there would be no avoiding the wedding.

"I'm fine," she said again. "I think it maybe just got a little hot in here. Maybe we should get some air."

Jenny nodded and after a quick word to the sales lady, who started bundling Marissa's dress into a garment bag, they walked out into the warm summer day.

"Are you feeling better now?"

Marissa nodded. "I'll be okay." She said the words and let them sink in. Of course she would be okay.

Everything with Nick was a long time ago and she was a different person now.

Stronger, more confident and...no longer in love with Nick Slater.

Yes. She'd be fine as long as she just kept lying to herself.

"So you're really going to do it, hey?" Nick Slater slapped his best friend on the back in way of a greeting.

Jake immediately spun around and pulled Nick into a bro hug. "You made it."

"Of course I made it." Nick dropped his duffel bag on the

floor of the hotel lobby. "I wouldn't miss this, man. I mean, it's not every day your best friend gets married." He nudged Jake in the ribs. "At least it better not be."

"No way." Jake shook his head. "Jenny is the one for me. The only one. I'm only doing this once."

"That's a good thing, because I can't imagine you'd find two women to agree to marry you." Nick laughed and ducked Jake's punch. "Where is the love of your life anyway? I haven't seen Jenny in far too long."

"Maybe if you didn't work so much we'd actually see you."

Nick knew it wasn't intentional, but Jake's comments hit home. He'd been so busy working for his father's manufacturing company for the last few years, taking on the role of sourcing parts, mostly overseas, he hadn't spent nearly as much time at home with his friends and family as he would have liked. The fact that he almost missed his best friend's wedding because of meetings in China had been a wake-up call.

A big one.

Important meetings or not, he wasn't going to miss Jake and Jenny's wedding. And when he'd told his father that was his reason for leaving before securing the manufacturing deal they needed, well...he wasn't even sure he was going to have a job to return to when the weekend was over. Not that he was going to waste too much time thinking about it. After all, there was nothing he could do about it now.

Might as well enjoy the wedding and celebrate the man who had always been more like a brother than just a friend. In fact, the entire Duncan family had always made him feel more at home and accepted than his own. It had been Jake's dad, Alan, who'd taught him how to fish while his own dad had been too busy working. Jake's mom, Patrice, who'd sat with him for hours until he finally under-stood geometry in the tenth grade. And then there was

Missy, who'd been just like his own little sister. Together, Jake and Nick had teased and tormented her until one day the teasing stopped and...

Missy.

"Hey. I was kidding." Jake punched him in the shoulder, pulling him out of his thoughts. "Sort of. But I am glad you're back. I couldn't do this without you."

"Sure you could." Nick picked up his bag and together they walked toward the front desk so he could check in. "You just wouldn't want to."

"You got that right. As of tomorrow, I'll have all my favorite people here. The girls are on their way. They had some last-minute dress fittings or something."

"The girls?" Nick asked before giving the desk attendant his information and credit card to secure his room.

"Yeah. And wait until you see the bridesmaid dress. Marissa is going to kill me, but it was way too good of a—"

"Missy?" Nick knew he sounded like an idiot and he probably looked even more idiotic but he couldn't help it. Of course, he knew on some level that Missy would be there. It was her brother's wedding after all, but he hadn't really thought about what that would actually mean. "She's here?"

Jake shook his head and blinked hard. "Are you drunk, man? No. I just told you that the girls had dress fittings. And you really should stop calling her Missy. She hated it when we were kids, and I can't imagine she'll like it any better now."

"When are they getting here?" Nick ignored the comment about Marissa's nickname. He'd always called her Missy; it was their special thing. Or at least, it had been. She protested, but Nick was pretty sure she secretly liked it.

"They'll be here later. In time for dinner."

"Tonight?"

Jake nodded slowly. "That's right. Tonight. At the dinner with the families and the bridal party. You got the email I sent you with all the details for the weekend, right?"

Nick vaguely remembered an itinerary with all the bridal activities, but he hadn't paid much attention to it because he was busy trying to actually make it to the wedding. He figured Jake and Jenny could fill him in on all the particulars once he got here. "Maybe you can fill me in?" He shrugged apologetically before he accepted the key and information the front desk clerk handed him.

Jake shook his head and laughed. "I'll get you a new copy of the itinerary. Jenny worked hard to make this a whole destination wedding thing. So we have a few days of activities planned for everyone."

"Seriously?"

"Absolutely."

"Anything I need to know about? Or can I just lay low until Saturday?"

His buddy chuckled and they walked through the grand timber-framed lobby toward the bank of elevators. "I'll email you the itinerary right away so you can brush up before dinner or Jenny might just kill you. You should know better than to piss off a bride. She seems super sweet and all, but..."

"Ha! I can't believe Jenny would get bridezilla. You maybe, but not Jenny."

They laughed together as Jake walked with him up to his room and Nick knew he'd made the right decision. Even if it meant his dad disowning him and kicking him out of the family business, there was nowhere he'd rather be than next to his best friend, laughing, joking, and helping him prepare for the most important day of his life.

The Duncan family meant too much to him.

"This is your room," Jake said as they approached a door at the end of the hall. "I hope you don't mind, but we had to switch up a few of the reservations when we were block booking the rooms."

"What do you mean?" Nick held up the key to the door and heard a click as the lock released.

"So you actually have a two-bedroom suite," Jake said as they walked into the incredible room. Instantly, they were greeted with a picture window that looked out at the mountain range, making it feel as if the mountain were right in the room with them.

"A suite?" Nick dropped his bag on a chair and walked around the impressive room. Sure enough, there were two doors leading to what must have been the bedrooms. "Okay. It's a little much for just me, but whatever works."

"That's the thing," Jake said. "The room was initially for some of Jenny's cousins, but there was a bit of a fight between the women, and they refuse to share the space, so I had to give them two separate rooms and because it all happened really quickly, I figured that the best two people to share the suite were you and Marissa. I mean, you're practically brother and sister anyway, right? So you grab a room and she'll take the other one."

"What?" Jake was so casual about him sharing a room with his little sister that it took Nick a moment to realize what he'd actually said. "You want me to share a room with Missy?"

"No."

Nick tried not to look visibly relieved. He hadn't seen her for eight years, but he was pretty sure she wasn't going to be any happier to see him. Sharing space with her would only make things more awkward.

"Not a *room*," Jake said. "A suite. You'll each have your own rooms. It's not a big deal, is it? Because you guys are practically related, so it shouldn't be weird or anything."

Of course it *shouldn't* be weird.

Maybe if Jake knew that his little sister had kissed him

seconds after declaring her feelings for him, he'd feel differently.

But he didn't.

Just like he didn't know that Nick had broken her heart all those years ago in the cruelest way he knew how to do.

Just like he didn't know that the reason Nick had been such an asshole to her was because he, too, had feelings, and they scared the hell out of him.

Just like he didn't know that Nick had thought about Marissa every day for eight years and wondered what could have been different.

2

*M*arissa and Jenny were later getting out of the city than they'd planned and of course, traffic never cooperated when you were in a hurry. So by the time they got to the Lodge, a full two hours after they were scheduled to arrive, and approximately a mere twenty minutes before the family dinner was scheduled to start, Jenny was a frazzled mess.

"It's all good." Marissa tried in vain to calm her down. "You can't get so worked up this early in the weekend. I mean, way bigger things are going to—"

Marissa stopped talking when Jenny's eyes grew wide. Maybe her approach wasn't really the best one.

She tried again. "How about you go to your room and freshen up and I'll go make sure everything is organized for the dinner?"

"You'd do that?"

"Of course I will." What Marissa really wanted to do was go find her own room and freshen up herself, but sacrifices had to be made, and after all, that's what she was there for. "I'm the maid of honor, Jenny. I'll do whatever it takes to make sure your wedding is as beautiful as you. That's a promise."

The smile on her sister-in-law to-be's face was totally worth it, so Marissa left her bags with the bellhop, saw Jenny off in the direction of the exclusive chalets where Jake had secured them a special suite, and went in search of the restaurant where the dinner was to be hosted.

Marissa's mom and dad were already at the restaurant, just as she knew they would be. Her parents were always early. In fact, they'd already been at the Lodge for three days early, to have a little bit of a holiday before the wedding started.

"Marissa!" Her mom jumped up and gave her a hug as soon as she walked in. "You look tired, dear. Did you just get here?"

"We did." She finished hugging her mom and moved in to greet her dad.

"You look great, kiddo." He kissed her on the forehead and winked at her before releasing her.

Marissa knew she probably did look tired. She *was* tired.

"I didn't mean it like that," her mother protested and smacked her husband's arm playfully when she saw his grin. She waved him away and focused her attention on her daughter. "Where's Jenny? Jake said you were coming up together after a final dress fitting."

"Oh yes." She shook her head. "The dress fitting."

"It went well?"

"Let's just say, I'll have some words for my brother dearest. But Jenny's happy with it all, so that's all that matters."

Her mother gave her a strange look but didn't push any further.

"We're running late, so Jenny just went back to the room to freshen up quickly before dinner. I'm supposed to make sure everything is on track with the dinner. I should probably go find the hostess to make sure everything's good. Can you do me a favor and make sure the place cards are set out properly?"

"Of course, dear. Whatever you need."

"Thanks." She gave her mom a quick squeeze. They'd always been a close family and it was nice to know her mom had her back. Marissa handed her mom the packet Jenny had given her that had the name cards and the seating plan. The woman was so organized, Marissa couldn't imagine what she could possibly be stressed about, but then again, Marissa wasn't the one getting married.

She found the hostess by the bar, introduced herself and for the next few minutes chatted about the menu and wine selections. Again, Jenny had taken care of all the details and there really wasn't much for Marissa to worry about. She made sure the woman knew what the bride and groom looked like so they'd be well taken care of. Satisfied that everything would go smoothly, she popped into the restroom to touch up her makeup as best as she could. She ran her fingers through her hair and applied a bit of lip gloss in an effort to look slightly less as though she'd just hopped out of the car before she returned to the table where her mom had done her job.

"It'll be so nice to see Nick again, won't it?" her mom said to her when she walked up. "It's been so long. He's just been so busy with that job of his. When was the last time you saw him, Marissa?"

She didn't want to tell her mom that it had been almost eight years since she'd laid eyes on Nick Slater, because she fully knew what her mother's reaction would be. She would be horrified. As far as everyone in their family was concerned, Nick was like another son, another older brother to Marissa. Everyone felt that way, except for Marissa. She'd never hear the end of it.

Marissa shrugged. "I don't know," she said. "It's been awhile, for sure. We've just all been busy and I'm sure he has his own life, too." What she didn't say was that she was sure he must have a girlfriend or be busy dating or otherwise keeping himself entertained.

It surprised her how, even after eight years, the idea of Nick with another woman hurt. Marissa took a breath and pulled herself together. She couldn't afford to be all weird tonight. She was going to see Nick and she needed to just act as if nothing had happened. It was the only way she would be able to get through the wedding weekend. And really, nothing *had* happened. She was being ridiculous and they were both completely different people, so it shouldn't matter.

"Well, you'll be able to catch up tonight," her mother said. "You're sitting next to each other."

"What?"

Her mom pointed to the table and the name cards that were laid out perfectly. "I put them out just like Jenny's seating chart said. You're both over there."

Oh no. That was not going to happen. It was bad enough that she had to pretend to be okay when her insides felt as though they were made completely of Jell-O, but there was no way she was going to torture herself by sitting next to him all night. It was too much, too soon.

Marissa didn't bother excusing herself before she made her way over to the end of the table where her mom had pointed. She grabbed her name card and was just about to swap it with someone on the other end of the room when a familiar voice froze her in place.

"Missy."

*S*HE LOOKED GOOD.

Nick spotted her the moment he walked into the restaurant. She wore simple black pants and a bright-blue silky top. It was simple, but somehow Marissa made it look dressed up.

Had she always been so sexy?

No. She'd been his best friend's little sister. Always around, cute, freckle-faced, but not sexy. At least, not until that's exactly what she was. Nick remembered the first time when he'd first noticed Missy as a woman and not as a little sister. She'd been fifteen; he was sixteen and somehow overnight she'd completely changed from a little girl into a woman. That was the beginning of the end, as far as Nick was concerned.

Every day after that had been an exercise in self-control.

And the wedding weekend was clearly not going to be an exception.

He took a deep breath and in that instant, almost as if she sensed him, Missy looked up. She was frowning at a piece of paper she held in her hands, but when her eyes met his, the frown fell away. Her lips formed a little *O.* She glanced down quickly at the paper in her hand and then back to Nick.

He smiled because how could he not when he saw her? Despite the awkwardness between them, there was also so much more. A lifetime of history. And it was good to see her. *So* very good.

"Missy."

Her mouth twitched at the use of her nickname and she shook her head slightly. But she smiled.

Nick crossed the room to her and moved to give her a hug, but he stopped himself. It was still weird. Which was crazy, because all he wanted to do was have her in his arms. Instead, he crossed his arms over his chest. "It's good to see you."

"You, too," she said. "I didn't think you were coming. Something about a meeting overseas."

"There's no way I could miss Jake's wedding. Disappointed?"

"That you're here?"

He challenged her with his eyes, needing to get a read on how she felt about things with them. It had been eight years, after all; there was no way she could still have feelings for him or be upset in any way about that night. But he couldn't read anything in her eyes.

"No," she said. "I know it means a lot to Jake that you're here."

"And you?"

Nick didn't know what he expected her to say to such a bold question, but he couldn't help himself. But she didn't answer. Instead, she glanced again at the paper in her hands and held it up. "Looks like we're sitting next to each other."

Before he could say anything to that, Patrice's voice cut through. A moment later, he was embraced in the woman's hug. "Nick. It's been way too long," she said. "You've just been working way too hard. Your dad must think he's won the lottery having you at his side."

"Well, I don't know about that," he said good-naturedly. "But you are right about one thing—it's been way too long since I've had the pleasure of spending time with the Duncan family." He turned to include Missy in the statement but she was gone. He felt the immediate sense of loss, which was ridiculous because this time, unlike the last time he saw her, he knew she couldn't have gone far.

Nick spent the next forty-five minutes catching up with Mr. and Mrs. Duncan, meeting and charming Jenny's family members, and of course joking with the bride and groom when they arrived. Missy was absent for the first half of the cocktail hour, and when she did make her appearance, it was clear, at least to Nick, that she was purposely talking to people who were on the opposite side of the room from him.

When the waitress appeared to announce that dinner was about to be served, he took his seat and glanced at the name tag at the place setting next to him. She wouldn't be able to avoid him for long.

Sure enough, moments before the salads were placed in

front of them, Missy slid into her seat and fluffed the napkin over her lap.

"Avoiding me?"

Her head snapped over and she glared at him for an instant. "Why would I do that? I'm simply being a good hostess and fulfilling my maid of honor duties."

"Is that all it was?" He couldn't help but poke at her. It was so easy to fall into the old habits of teasing her. Even if everything was different now. "Because I could have sworn you were avoiding me."

"Nick, could you tell us all about what China is like?" Patrice asked him from across the table, once again distracting him from the woman he really wanted to talk to. "I think Jenny's father has been there, isn't that right, Bruce?" She gestured to Jenny's dad to bring him into the discussion and they fell into easy conversation about China and Nick's other travels. Missy was notably quiet, but despite her silence, Nick was very much aware of her nearness. The urge to reach his hand over to hers was strong and completely unreasonable as he had no right to touch her.

They didn't have that kind of relationship.

Heck, he didn't know what kind of relationship they had. The easiness between them that they shared as kids was gone. It would likely never be back. And judging by how it made him feel just to see her again, Nick was pretty sure he didn't want that brother/sister relationship back again. The feelings he'd had eight years ago, the ones he thought he'd squashed, were still very much there.

3

———

*I*t was pretty much torture to have to sit so close to Nick Slater for the entire evening. Sure, the most humiliating night of her life had been a long time ago, but that didn't change how she felt about him.

It should have.

Time and distance should have changed everything.

But the minute Nick walked into that restaurant and called her by that annoying nickname he had for her, it all came back. Every single feeling she'd ever had crashed back so hard she'd almost fallen over.

If it hadn't been for the table to support her, she might have done just that.

How was it possible to still have feelings for the man? They'd been kids the last time she saw him. He'd humiliated her. Broken her heart. Crushed her.

She should hate him.

But she didn't.

Marissa spent the evening listening to his easy conversation, the way he made everyone feel special and included in the conversation, and the casual ease he carried himself with.

Marissa realized that not only did she not hate Nick, she actually really liked him. A lot.

Probably too much.

Repeatedly through the night, she forced herself to take deep breaths and stay calm. Things had changed over the years. She wasn't a child anymore. She was a successful real estate agent with a flourishing career, her own house and an active social life. There was no reason for her to be insecure or in any way intimidated by Nick or their past.

She just needed to get through the weekend and she'd be fine. She could go back to living her life and never having to see him again.

"Marissa, did you and Nick have a chance to go over the itinerary?"

She shook her head and blinked hard at Jenny, who had moved so she sat next to Marissa. "The what?"

"The itinerary? For the weekend? Remember, I sent it to you last week so you could familiarize yourself with it."

"Oh." Marissa did vaguely remember reading the email and glancing through the list of activities and events Jenny had planned. But she'd assumed she could just go with the flow when the time came. "I looked at it."

"Oh good," Jenny said. "So you and Nick will have a chance to organize the games for tomorrow. You're team captains, after all."

"Right." She had no idea what Jenny was talking about, but Marissa had the distinct feeling that if she admitted that, Jenny might burst into tears. She'd been so strong and put together up until the car ride up to the Lodge. Now, she seemed like a typical, overstressed, completely nervous bride and Marissa was not going to be the one responsible for causing her to have a breakdown. Besides, she had the capability of digging up the email to figure out what Jenny was talking about. "We're definitely going to take care of it." Nick looked over in her direction, and she did her best to give him a look that indicated she needed full agreement. "Aren't we, Nick?"

To his credit, it only took Nick a second to figure out what was going on. Or at least that Marissa needed agreement. He quickly nodded and wrapped his arm around Marissa's shoulders, giving them a squeeze. "Absolutely," he said. "Missy and I have this totally under control."

She tried to breathe and to not go completely stiff, but the fact that Nick Slater had his arm around her was almost paralyzing. He smelled so good; the weight of his arm felt safe in a way that didn't even make sense and when he squeezed her close, her stomach did a little flip.

Marissa swallowed hard.

"I just love the way he calls you Missy." Jenny grinned. "Jake said you all were like siblings growing up and I can see just how much you care about each other." She pulled them into a quick group hug. "I'm so glad you both are standing up for us. I can't think of two people more perfect for the job. And you'll have time to work on your dance since you're sharing a room. I'm so sorry about that situation." Jenny kept talking, as if she hadn't just dropped a bomb. "But my cousins can be so ridiculous sometimes. Best friends one minute and archenemies the next. You would think they could sort themselves out before my—"

"What did you say?" Marissa interrupted her. Nick's arm was still wrapped around her, but the weight of it no longer felt safe. It felt...*dangerous*. In a way that meant her heart may be completely at risk if she wasn't careful. "About sharing a room?"

Jenny looked quickly between them. "Nick didn't tell you?"

"Haven't had a chance." Nick shrugged and Marissa would've smacked him if she could have freed her arm in time. "Don't worry, Jenny. I'll fill Missy in on all the details."

Yes. She was definitely going to punch him.

"Thank you." Jenny looked visibly relieved so Marissa made a mental note not to punch anyone in the bride's presence. Even Nick.

And then just like that, she was gone.

The minute they were alone, Marissa wiggled away from him and spun to face Nick. "What do you mean we're sharing a room?"

"It's not really like we're sharing a *room*. It's a two-bedroom suite. You still have your own bed. Don't worry."

She opened her mouth but no words came out.

"And besides, it will give us time to work on this dance Jenny was talking about. Jake did say something about how they wanted the dances to look good. So maybe we should practice?"

Marissa opened and shut her mouth, but *still* no words came out. It was bad enough being in the same hotel as Nick—how on earth was she going to survive sharing a room with him?

"Missy, watch your face." Nick winked at her. "You look a bit like a guppy out of water right now."

Nick read the itinerary and then read it again. He really should have paid more attention to it earlier. He sank into the chair by the window and looked again at Missy's closed bedroom door.

After the dinner was over, Missy dragged her feet about going back to the room, and she tried to be sneaky when she went to the front desk to request a new room, but Nick noticed.

It was strange, but he was a little hurt that she was so bothered about sharing a suite with him. It's not like they were sharing a *room,* after all. And really, they'd been friends for most of their life; it shouldn't be a big deal.

But it was.

He'd be lying if he said it wasn't a big deal for him too.

Nick thought he would be fine, but when he saw Marissa standing there, everything he thought he'd feel went totally out the window. Apparently not even eight years was enough to make those feelings disappear. She was even more beautiful than before, and something about the easy way she laughed tugged at something low in his gut.

He pulled his gaze away from her bedroom door and back at the itinerary. She'd already been in there over twenty minutes. But there was no way she'd gone to bed. They had too much to do. This wedding was definitely an action-packed weekend.

There was no help for it; he was going to have to knock. He put his paper down, took a breath and stood. His hand was poised over the door, ready to knock, when it opened.

Missy stood in front of him in sweatpants and tank top, her hair up in a ponytail. Her face had been washed and she looked...gorgeous.

"I was just about to see if you were in bed."

That did not come out right.

She looked at first shocked and then she laughed. "Were you now?"

"Not like that." Nick held up his hands and laughed along with her. "I was just looking at the plans for the weekend and I thought maybe we should organize a few things."

Her face relaxed and she moved past him into the room. "Jenny does seem to have every moment planned and accounted for," she said. "I do like how organized she is, but still...I think I'll need a vacation when all this is over." She flopped down on the couch and grabbed the piece of paper from the table.

Nick had to resist the urge to go sit next to her and put his arm around her to pull her into a cuddle. It felt natural to do so, but at the same time...there was no way.

He made a point to sit on the other side of the room, in the same chair he'd been in.

"So what's first?" Missy read down the list. "Oh yes, it looks like we're going to be team captains tomorrow for wedding wars. I hope you're ready to get taken down?"

"In a tug-of-war?" He laughed. "There's no way your team is going to beat mine." He flexed as a joke, but he didn't miss the way her eyes widened seconds before she looked away.

It was ludicrous to even believe that Missy was still attracted to him. And even if she was, there was no way she would even *like* him anymore. He'd done his best to take care of that the night she confessed her feelings to him.

He still remembered it as if it had just happened yesterday. It was her graduation night, and she'd looked amazing in her black fitted dress, with a slit up her thigh and a dangerously low-cut back. Having graduated a year before her, Nick and Jake were both home from college and, after the Duncans' celebratory BBQ, had been lingering around as Missy and her friends got ready for the graduation dance.

When their dates arrived to pick them up, Jake and Nick gave the boys a hard time. Nick focused on Missy's date in particular. It should have been him who took her to her dance. For almost three years, he'd secretly wished it would somehow be him. But Jake would have killed him. There was a code, and there was no way Nick could break it. No matter what. The Duncan family had been more like a family to him than his own; he couldn't screw it up by dating Missy.

And that's why, when later that night, Missy came home from her dance and found Nick in the kitchen getting a glass of water, he had to do the hardest thing he'd ever done in his life.

She'd looked amazing when she'd walked over to him, and no doubt she'd seen his own desire reflected in his eyes. He'd never forget what she said: "Nick, I know I shouldn't, but I think tonight is the perfect night to tell you that I'm in love with you. I have been for years." And then she kissed him. And he kissed her back. And it was the single most amazing kiss he'd ever had, or had since.

It had taken every bit of willpower he possessed not to pull her close and deepen that kiss, but instead to push her away and —it still made him cringe to think about it—laugh at her. He'd called her a silly little girl and he'd *laughed*. Nick would never forget the look on Missy's face as she realized what he was doing. She'd been devastated.

And he'd done it to her.

Little did she know that he'd crushed his own heart as well.

But it had been for the best. Jake would never have forgiven him.

That had been eight years ago. Looking at the confident woman in front of him now, there was no way he could believe that she could have any feelings left for him, not after the way he'd hurt her.

"What do you think?" she asked him and he realized he had been lost in his memories and hadn't heard a word she'd said.

"About what?"

"The dance." Missy grinned at him. "Jenny and Jake have been practicing their first dance for months, and she made it very clear that we were supposed to look good on the dance floor as well."

"So we need to practice?"

"I think that's the idea." Missy popped up from the couch and grabbed her phone. "I downloaded the song—just let me find it."

While she was looking through her phone, Nick got to work clearing the furniture out of the way. He was just pushing the couch back when the song started to play.

"You've got to be kidding me." He shook his head with a laugh because the song Jenny and Jake had picked for them to dance to had to be a joke.

"I'M PRETTY sure my brother has decided to use his wedding to play one giant practical joke on me," Marissa said. "You should see my dress."

"Your dress?"

"You'll see." She shook her head.

"But this song?"

The song was the iconic "(I've Had) The Time of My Life" from *Dirty Dancing*, a movie Marissa had loved and forced the boys to watch multiple times with her when they were growing up. It wasn't her favorite song from the movie, but more than once when she was a teenager she'd fantasized about dancing with Nick to it. In fact, more times than she'd like to count.

But there was no way Jake could know that.

"I don't think we have to enact the actual dance from the movie." She laughed even though she'd imagined it in her head enough times that she could probably pull it off. "We're just supposed to look...seamless."

Nick held out his arms; Marissa hesitated, but only for a second. She could do this. She could handle Nick Slater's arms holding her close.

She could.

She stepped closer and his arms closed around her. Marissa tried not to breathe in the scent of him. He smelled like cedar and orange, just the way he always had. She closed her eyes to keep from looking at him.

"You okay?"

She nodded, not trusting her voice, and he started to move in time to the music.

They'd never danced together before—unless you counted her dreams, and she didn't. But despite their inexperience together, they moved around the small living room as if they'd done it a million times and Marissa lost herself in the moment.

When the song ended, she was dizzy, but not because of the dancing. The feelings that flooded through her knocked her completely off guard. It was one thing to see Nick Slater across the room for the first time in so long. It was another to sit by him at dinner and share a suite with him. But it was a completely different thing altogether to be in his arms, dancing to a song she'd fantasized about since she was sixteen.

She couldn't help it. It didn't make sense, and nothing about it was a good idea, but there was no denying it. Even after almost a decade, she was still in love with Nick Slater.

"Missy?"

Her eyes fluttered open to see Nick looking down at her with concern on his face. Their faces were so close. Only inches apart really. She could kiss him. She could reach up on her tippy-toes and kiss him, just the way she had before.

Remember how that ended up?

"Are you okay?"

"Yes," she answered quickly. "I'm fine. I'm just...I'm tired I think. It's been a long day." She pulled out of his embrace and put distance between them. She hadn't imagined the connection. There was no way that was her imagination. He'd felt it too; he had to. She could see it in his eyes, feel it in his touch. Just the way she had all those years ago when she'd been so sure he felt the same way she did.

But you were wrong.

The voice in her head was starting to become very annoying.

"Why don't you sit down?" he said. "I can get you a glass of—"

"No." She wrapped her arms around her, suddenly cold without his embrace. "I should probably just go to bed. After all,

I need to be rested if my team is going to kick your team's butt tomorrow."

He laughed and the weird moment was gone.

Mostly.

"Whatever you need to tell yourself," he said. "But Team Groom is still going to win."

"Ha."

She couldn't think of anything else to say, so she lifted her hand in an awkward wave and slipped into her room without even saying goodnight.

The minute there was a door between them, she slid to the floor and dropped her head onto her knees. *This couldn't be happening. It just couldn't.* She couldn't possibly still be in love with him. It was ridiculous. She was a grown woman, for goodness' sake. She was no longer a silly teenager with unrealistic expectations about falling in love with her brother's best friend.

She'd dated other guys. Heck, she'd been in love with other men.

Sort of.

Not like Nick.

Never like Nick.

"Get a hold of yourself, Marissa," she whispered into her knees. "It's only three days." She could handle being around him for three days. Of course she could and then she could go back to avoiding him again for the next eight years. At least.

He doesn't love you. Move on. He doesn't love you.

It was a mantra she forced herself to say in her head over and over again, when she was eighteen in those days and weeks following her humiliation. She had to get it through her head despite what she thought. Despite all the indications and signals she'd gotten from him. The way he looked at her, the way his hand would *accidentally* reach out and brush her arm. The way he'd spend extra time talking to her about school and the future.

The way he'd go out of his way to take her to work or pick her up from a friend's house, even if it messed up his plans with Jake. The way, even for a moment, he'd kissed her back and slipped his hand around her so it was resting on her bare back that night in the kitchen when she'd thrown all caution to the wind and declared her love for him.

Despite all those things that made her think that maybe, just maybe, he loved her too. He didn't. He'd made that very, very clear.

"Missy, you're such a silly little girl," he'd said. He pushed her away from him and laughed.

She'd never forget that laugh because it went right to her heart, cracking it in two.

Marissa remembered standing there, waiting for a moment for him to say sorry and tell her that he didn't mean it and that he did love her. But he hadn't.

So she'd turned and ran to her room to cry her heart out, Nick's words replaying over in her head on a cruel, vicious loop.

No. She would not subject herself to that kind of hurt and humiliation again.

This time she would just keep her feelings to herself.

4

---

*T*he next morning, Nick waited for Missy as long as he could before leaving the suite to go in search of breakfast. He had to stop himself from knocking on her door to see whether she'd like to join him. Somehow it didn't feel right to disturb her.

The night before, holding her in his arms and dancing to what he knew was one of her favorite songs from one of her favorite movies of all time, it had felt so...well, it had felt *right*. But it wasn't.

Nothing had changed. Missy was still Jake's little sister. That would never change.

Besides, the odds that she still felt the same way about him after so many years were slim. She was a beautiful, successful woman. There was no way she was still hung up on him. Heck, it was entirely likely she had a boyfriend.

But if she did, where was he?

Stop it.

Nick forced himself to stop thinking about Missy in any other term besides little sister and maid of honor, and he focused his attentions on the task at hand.

Which, as far as he was concerned, was getting some breakfast.

He found Jake and his parents in the dining room. "Good morning." He slid into a seat next to Patrice. "Is everyone ready for today's activities?"

"The real question is, are you?" Jake pointed a piece of toast at him before he took a bite. "I know Jenny has you and Marissa in charge of leading the teams. Are you up for it?"

"Brother..." Nick poured himself a cup of coffee. "Anything you need from me, I've got it. I *am* your best man, after all. I have this well under control."

"Well, I think it's so nice that Jenny and Jake have organized so much fun this weekend. It really turns the wedding into a bit more of an event, don't you think?"

Nick nodded, although he wasn't so sure how doing a scavenger hunt and competing in a couple of games was much of an event, but there was no way he was going to say anything.

"And, it looks like I'm on Team Groom," Patrice said. "Alan is on Team Bride, so we better make sure we win."

She winked at her husband, who blew her a kiss in return.

Nick had always been envious of the Duncans' easy marriage. They just seemed to really love each other, and they always had. Unlike his own parents, who seemed to moderately tolerate each other—when they weren't bickering, that was.

The Slaters had definitely not been the model of marriage, or family. Or really much of anything except for how to run a successful business, which reminded Nick—no doubt his voicemail was full of angry messages from his father about the cancelled meeting.

He didn't care.

Not really.

He'd listen to them later and assess the damage then. There wasn't much he could do about it at the moment anyway. Especially when his best friend was counting on him to help make his wedding an *event*.

"Not to worry," Nick said. "Team Groom is definitely going to beat Missy."

Patrice gave him a strange look but didn't say anything because at that moment, Jenny joined them and said, "I don't think so, Nick. Team Bride has this locked up. I have full confidence in Marissa on this."

"Where is Marissa anyway?" It was Jake who asked him, but all Nick could do was shrug. He didn't want to tell them that he'd waited most of the morning for her to come out of her room, or that they'd left things awkwardly the night before after dancing together in the living room. So he just shrugged again and grabbed a piece of toast from the plate in the center of the table.

Patrice exchanged a look with her husband, but nobody said anything else about the matter until it was time to head out to the games.

"Hey." Jake grabbed his arm and pulled him to the side away from the group as they walked down the corridor and out to the courtyard. "I just wanted to thank you."

"For what?"

"For being my best man, of course."

Nick waved him away. "As if anyone else could possibly do the job."

"You're right about that." Jake laughed. "But I know it's probably not easy to do this with Marissa."

Nick froze. "What do you mean?" *There was no way Jake could know about his feelings for Missy.* He'd done his best to hide them for years. It was the one thing he'd never told his best friend. The one thing he'd kept from him to protect their relationship. "Why would it be hard?"

"Because she's my *sister*." Jake laughed. "And Marissa can be a little...well...she's my *sister,* man." Jake laughed and Nick joined in.

"You know I love Missy," he said. "It's nice to be able to spend some time with her again. It'll be fun."

"It will be fun." Jake slapped him on the back. "We better go before Jenny docks Team Groom for being late."

MARISSA WAS ready and waiting in the courtyard long before anyone showed up for the games. In fact, she'd been ready for hours, having woken up extra early to get out of the suite before Nick woke up. After the dance the night before, Marissa decided it would be best to limit any time that she had to spend alone with Nick. It might help with the feelings that, much to her dismay, had definitely not faded in the last eight years.

It *might* help.

So far, it had just given her extra time awake, when all she could do was think about Nick. The games would be good. They would distract her. That's what she needed: a distraction.

Except the moment the glass doors opened and Nick, along with the rest of her family and a handful of other wedding guests, spilled out into the courtyard, Marissa's stomach did that annoying flip thing it had been doing since the night before whenever Nick was around.

"There you are," Nick said when he approached. "Where were you this morning? I waited for a long time but hunger got the best of me and I had to come downstairs."

"Oh." She tried to sound casual. "I couldn't sleep so I thought I'd just get a jump on the day."

"You mean you weren't even there?"

She shook her head and handed him a list. "Here's the

agenda for the morning. We'll start with the scavenger hunt and then finish with tug-of-war."

"And the teams?"

She handed him another list. "They've been assigned." Marissa did her best to keep her voice neutral. She hadn't failed to notice how a handful of Jenny's single and eligible cousins had been put on Nick's team. She also hadn't failed to notice how they'd been sitting in the corner, giggling and pointing at Nick since he'd arrived.

It shouldn't bother her, but it did. She made a point of turning away from the cousins as she consulted her own list. "I'm going to gather my team," she told Nick. "I have Jenny's brother and his wife. She looks strong, so we'll definitely win." She tried to sound casual. "Will you be ready to get started in a few minutes?"

"Sure." He looked up from his list and nodded. Marissa turned away to leave, but Nick grabbed her arm. "Hey," he said. "Maybe we could...I don't know...work on our speeches later?"

"Speeches?"

"You know, for the reception. We both have to give speeches. I thought maybe it would be kind of fun to bounce some ideas off each other."

She watched him for a minute, trying to find something in his eyes that would give her an indication of why he might be trying so hard to spend time with her. If she didn't know better, she might think that maybe he was interested in her. But that was ridiculous.

Was it?

Even if it wasn't...

"Okay." She said yes before she realized what she'd said. "That would be fun."

It would? She really needed to get away from him before she declared her undying love for him next.

"I should..." She gestured to the group of family members. "Get my..." She shrugged, aware that she probably sounded like an idiot.

"Go," he said, excusing her. "Get your team ready and let's get this started."

She nodded and moved away, silently cursing herself. *What was it about the man that made her so tongue-tied?* It was ridiculous.

"Ready for this?" Marissa's dad patted her on the back and slipped the list from her hand. "I think I have most of our team assembled and they're excited."

She laughed, successfully distracted from the effect of Nick. "You're really getting into this, Dad."

"Damn straight. Your mother seems to think that Nick is going to lead them to victory, but I believe in you, Marissa."

She shook her head and laughed again. "Whatever you say, Dad. But it will be a team effort. Go gather the troops. I'll get the lists ready."

A few minutes later, her father had rounded up the team and Marissa gave the instructions. "Okay," she said to her small assembled group. "It's a photo scavenger hunt. Dad is passing out the lists." She gestured to her dad, who was happily handing the papers out. "Use your cell phones to take pictures of every-thing on the list and for every team member we have who completes the list, we get a point. Make sense?"

Everyone nodded their heads, excited to get going.

"Great," Marissa said. "Let's meet back here in twenty minutes to add up the points. Have fun and go Team Bride!"

There were a few hoots and hollers as everyone dispersed with their cell phones and lists.

She couldn't help but notice that Nick's team had already disappeared. Normally, she wasn't a very competitive person. Maybe it was the situation—maybe it was Nick? Whatever it was, she wanted desperately for Team Bride to wipe the floor with Nick and his group.

She waited until everyone had happily scattered in various directions and consulted her own list to see what she could take care of quickly.

A picture of the wedding site.

She could do that. It was right around the corner by the little pond and waterfall.

A wedding guest meeting someone new.

That was easy enough.

Cousins together.

Super easy.

Members of the bridal party kissing.

Marissa rolled her eyes. No doubt she was going to see more than she ever wanted of her brother kissing his new bride. Not that it wasn't great that he was in love—that *was* great. But she could definitely do without watching her big brother swap spit.

With a sigh, she tucked the list in her back pocket and headed off to get some of the easier pictures first.

It didn't take Marissa long to knock off the first few items off her list. She was just headed over to the ceremony site to take care of that one, when she heard voices. It looked as if half the guests were gathered there to get the photo, and maybe with a little luck the bride and groom—who had mysteriously disappeared right before the scavenger hunt had started, no doubt to make it hard to score the last shot—would be there.

But Jake and Jenny weren't there.

Instead, Nick was there, sitting on the rocks by the water with a few of Jenny's cousins, who were fawning all over him.

"Give up already?" she asked with a roll of her eyes. Marissa lifted her phone and took a picture of the ceremony site.

"On the contrary." Nick had jumped up and was standing

next to her when she lowered her phone. "I was just waiting for the winning picture."

"The what—"

Before she could finish her question, Nick wrapped his arms around her, and his mouth was on hers in a deep and completely unexpected kiss.

It took her a moment to realize what was happening, and by the time she did, every nerve ending in her body was on fire with the electricity coming from Nick's lips and the hottest kiss she'd ever had. Instinctually, Marissa slipped her hands around his back and kissed him right back.

It only took Nick about five seconds to forget what the purpose of the kiss was supposed to be. Only five seconds because as soon as he put his lips on her soft, sweet mouth, he was completely lost in her.

His body remembered eight years ago, a very similar kiss that had completely lit him up. Only this time, when Missy slid her arms around his back and deepened the kiss, Nick had no intention of pushing her away. And the very last thing he would do was laugh.

Because all he wanted to do was keep kissing her.

As long as possible.

A hoot sounded from somewhere nearby, but Nick didn't care. He slipped his tongue between her lips, in an effort to deepen the connection even further. Instantly, he wished he hadn't, because the spell was broken.

Missy's hands came up to his chest and she gave him a shove.

As he stumbled back a few steps, Nick was intensely aware of the absence of Missy in his arms. A few seconds later, he was also acutely aware of the way she was staring at him.

"What the hell, Nick?"

He had to think quickly. If he told her, right there, in front of everyone, how he'd wanted to do that from the moment he'd seen her in the dining room the night before, she'd get upset.

Hell, if he told her the truth—how he'd wanted to do that every day for the last eight years since their first and last kiss—she might kill him.

Nick shrugged and tucked his hands into his pockets. "We needed a kiss from members of the bridal party." He nodded his head toward Jenny's cousins, who stood nearby, holding their cell phones rather dumbly.

"A photo?"

He nodded and hated that he was lying to her. Because even though it was actually the truth, that had been the plan. Not to kiss Missy exactly, just anyone he saw first. He still hated the fact that he was diminishing what had just happened between them.

Because the truth was, it was more than just a photo for a contest. *Way* more. And he was a jerk for pretending that's all there was to it.

"And did you get what you needed?"

Audrey, Jenny's oldest cousin, nodded. "We did. Thank you. Now we have the whole list."

"Speaking of which." Nick made a show of looking at his watch. Anything to keep from looking at Missy. "We should get back. It's time to tally up the points."

She didn't look happy, but maybe she was still a little dazed from being kissed. Lord knew, Nick was more than dazed. He was completely shattered after that. It took all the focus he had just to put one foot in front of the other.

He waited a moment as Jenny's cousins left, headed back to the courtyard, before he turned to Marissa. "Hey, about that..."

"What?"

He shook his head. *She was not going to do that thing where she pretended nothing happened, was she?* Because something *had* happened. It most definitely had.

"You know, the...well, the..."

"The kiss?" She laughed and tossed her head back. "You got your point," she said. "And I guess you got one up on me. But Team Bride will still kick your ass in the tug-of-war." She flipped her hair back and started to walk away.

"That's not really what I meant," he called after her. It was lame and he knew it, but he couldn't seem to stop himself.

Missy stopped and turned around slowly. "What did you mean then?"

"Well..." He crossed the distance toward her and took her cell phone from her hand. "It's not really fair that we got the picture and you didn't. Let's get you one."

A look of horror crossed her face. She snatched her phone back before she stuffed it in her pocket. "I'm good, thanks. Like I said, we'll get you in the tug-of-war." And then she was gone, walking much faster than she had before, in the direction of the courtyard, away from him.

And his offer for another kiss.

He shouldn't feel rejected. After all, it was ridiculous and he'd covered up his intense desire with such a stupid guise. Not that it could be anything different.

Amazing kiss or not, Missy was still Jake's little sister.

And that was never going to change.

He took one more moment to pull himself together and followed in the direction the others had gone. He couldn't allow himself to get caught up in these feelings. After all, he still had best man wedding duties to perform.

That's what he was going to focus on. Because Jake deserved the greatest best man ever. Not one who was lusting after his little sister.

5

She wasn't sure how she survived it, but somehow Marissa got through the rest of the day and the games. Even without her scavenger hunt points, Team Bride came in first place with enough completed lists. The tug-of-war was a closer match, but Team Bride took it as well. She tried to meet Nick's eyes to gloat, but he kept his gaze averted.

In fact, for the rest of the day, he wouldn't look at her.

And he definitely didn't talk to her.

Even when they competed against each other in the three-legged race, he wouldn't make eye contact. After the bean bag toss, she stopped trying. And when Team Bride took the entire competition, squeaking out a slight victory after an intense arm wrestling match between her dad and Nick, she didn't even bother looking to him to gloat.

It was probably better that he didn't look at her anyway.

It was bad enough that every time she caught a glimpse of him, her entire body burned with the memory of how his mouth had felt on hers.

Damn.

It had taken eight years to get the memory of their first kiss out of her mind, and now she was going to have to start all over again.

Why had he done that? Why had he *kissed* her?

For the game. At least that's what he'd said.

That's all it was. She'd been telling herself that all day. And she'd keep telling herself that, too. At least until her brain believed it to be true.

There was nothing behind that kiss.

You're such a liar.

She was, too. Because there was definitely something behind that kiss. At least, there had been for her. The moment his lips touched hers, it was just like eight years ago. And as much as she tried to deny it, all those feelings she'd worked so hard to push down for eight years flooded back to the surface.

"Marissa." Jenny came up beside her. "Are you coming to dinner with us? I think we should toast our win, don't you?"

Marissa scanned the little group that had gathered. It was a mixture of family and friends, cousins and other wedding guests. There was no sign of Nick, but that didn't mean anything. No doubt he'd be close to Jake, or maybe Jenny's cousins.

The flicker of jealousy surprised her and she quickly shook it away.

"I don't know," she told Jenny. "It's been a big day and there's still more to come. I should probably get some rest."

Jenny pulled her into a quick, but tight hug. "I totally get it," she said. "I know that these weekend weddings can be intense, and I really do appreciate all your work on it. It means so much to have you here with me. After all, we're going to be sisters."

Marissa smiled and gave Jenny another hug. She really did like her sister-in-law to-be. She almost changed her mind to join them for dinner, Nick be dammed, but then she remembered she still had to work on an amazing Jenny-worthy speech for the wedding reception and that sealed the deal.

"I'm happy to do it," she said to Jenny. "But I think I'm just going to order some room service tonight and work on my speech. I want to make sure it's perfect."

"I'm sure it will be." Tears sprang to Jenny's eyes, but she was quick to wipe them away. "Everything about this wedding is going to be perfect."

Marissa couldn't help but think that was a lot of pressure to put on one day, but it definitely wasn't the time to say anything.

"It will be fantastic," she said instead. "Especially if I can go get to work." She grinned, and with one more quick hug, Jenny sent her on her way.

After a quick stop at the bar to order a chicken salad to be sent up to her room, Marissa was in the clear.

At least she hoped she was. There was a slight chance that Nick hadn't gone to the dinner either, but it was only a slight one. Nick never passed up a free dinner. Especially if there were beautiful women involved.

Again, the flare of jealousy lit in her gut, but she pushed it down again. She had no time for such petty thoughts. She'd promised Jenny an amazing speech, and that's just what she was going to get.

Marissa didn't even realize she'd been holding her breath as she opened the door to the suite, but as soon as she walked in, she exhaled.

Empty.

She didn't waste any time grabbing her laptop, pouring herself a glass of wine from the bottle in the fridge and setting up on the little balcony with her feet up. The view was breath-taking and definitely enough to inspire her. Besides, the Lodge was teeming with love and romantic vibes. It wouldn't be hard to write a heartfelt speech.

Soon enough, Marissa was completely immersed in her work. She didn't even notice the knock on her door, or the click as the door opened, or the footsteps that followed.

It wasn't until Nick stood directly in front of her, holding the room service tray in his hands, that Marissa noticed.

"WHAT ARE YOU DOING HERE?" Missy jumped up so fast her laptop almost went flying. Fortunately one hand caught it while the other flew to her chest.

"It's my room." He shrugged. "I didn't mean to scare you." And that was the truth. The last thing he'd meant to do was scare her. In fact, he'd been trying to avoid her. Nick's plan had been to sneak away from the group and back up to the room so he wouldn't have to torture himself by being so close to Missy. At least for one night.

He definitely hadn't planned to run into the room service guy, who stood dumbly in the hallway outside their room, holding a tray. Nick had no choice but to accept it and deliver it to Missy.

"I was bringing you your dinner." He raised the tray a little bit to make his point. "Which begs the question, why aren't you eating with the others?"

She put her laptop on the table next to her and reached for the tray, but Nick pulled it back, just out of reach while he waited for the answer.

"I could ask you the same question, you know?"

"You could," he conceded. "But it doesn't change the fact that I'm looking for an answer."

She sighed and pulled her hair back from her face before

letting it fall around her shoulders again. "I'm working on my speech for the wedding," she finally said. "Jenny has some pretty high expectations. I wanted to make sure I met them."

Nick handed her the tray, which she placed next to her laptop on the table. "I can understand that," he said. "That's actually the same reason I'm not at dinner."

It wasn't entirely true, but it also wasn't really a lie, either. Not that she needed to know that.

"Of course," she said, as if it was a perfectly reasonable explanation. "You'd have a speech as well." She moved closer to the tray on the table and lifted the lid for her meal. "Do you mind if I eat? I mean, you're welcome to stay...that's stupid. I'm sorry—it's your room, too. I just..."

"I know it's strange."

Missy put the tray down again and turned to face him. "No," she said. "Do you know what's strange?"

He shook his head, although he could definitely think of a few things.

"That kiss," she said. "That kiss was strange. Why would you do that? And don't tell me it was for the scavenger hunt."

"But..." He drifted away because he didn't know what else to tell her. Of course it *was* for the scavenger hunt, but it was mostly for him. Because ever since he'd set eyes on her again, the taste of her lips on his was the only thing he could think about. But he couldn't tell her that.

Or could he?

"It was for the scavenger hunt," he started to explain. But when he saw the disappointment that flashed in her eyes, just for a second before it disappeared, he grew bold. After all, there was nothing else to lose. "But it was mostly because from the moment I saw you yesterday, I've been wondering what it would be like to kiss you."

Her mouth fell open. She had definitely not been expecting

him to say that, which made sense because he hadn't been expecting to say it.

She shook her head, but there was no way he was going to let her walk away from this conversation. He took a step toward her, so he stood directly in front of her.

"Nick, I don't know...I can't...there really isn't—"

He silenced her with a kiss. This one deeper and more meaningful than the one earlier in the day. He wrapped his arms around her and pressed her close to him. She melted into the kiss easily, and this time she didn't push him away. When finally, he stepped back and pulled his lips softly off hers, he kept hold of her hand.

Alarm bells rang in his head. He shouldn't have done that. There was no way it was going to turn out okay. Missy was still *Missy*. She was still Jake's little sister. She was still off-limits.

But none of that mattered at that moment. Not with the way she was looking at him. A little smile lifted the corner of her lips and finally she spoke.

"Did that just happen?"

He nodded and returned the smile, pushing all of the worries and reasons they shouldn't be doing it out of his head. None of it mattered. "It certainly did. I hope it wasn't as strange as the one this afternoon, because this kiss was just for us."

She shook her head briefly. "No," she said. "There was definitely nothing strange about that."

Missy had to be thinking about the first time they'd kissed and the fallout from that moment. But if she was, she didn't say anything, which was fine by him. As far as Nick was concerned, none of that mattered anymore.

With her hand still in his, he pulled a chair close to hers and they sat. "How about we work on those speeches together? And maybe later we could—"

"Practice our dance again?"

He laughed. Yes, that was definitely a safer idea.

6

*A*fter an evening writing speeches and dancing around the living room, Marissa had gone to bed in an almost dream-like state. *Was it really possible that after all these years, they were finally coming together? Did they actually have a chance to be together?*

The question danced through her head as she tossed and turned and attempted to sleep.

Attempted because every time she closed her eyes, she remembered the kiss and relived every second of it. Like he'd said earlier, there was definitely nothing strange about that kiss. It wasn't done for others, just them.

They hadn't kissed again, but as far as Marissa was concerned, that was almost better because now there was an easiness between them that hadn't been there before. They laughed and joked, and the tension was gone.

When she was finally able to fall asleep, she fell into a deeply disturbing dream.

It was her wedding day. She walked down the aisle in the dress of her dreams, toward what had to be the man of her dreams. When he turned around, she could see it was Nick. Her heart swelled with happiness and then as she reached the altar, he began to laugh.

A cruel, heartless laugh. Just like he had all those years ago when she'd been so sure he loved her back. The laughter went on for what seemed like forever, as she simply stood there, crushed by the love of her life as he rejected her in the harshest way she could imagine, on her wedding day.

Marissa woke with a start to see the sun was starting to peek through her blinds. She sat up in bed and tried to process what had just happened.

It wasn't real.

They were past that. The laughing. The childishness. The rejection. That was in the past.

There was nothing funny about the way they'd kissed last night.

Things had definitely shifted between them. Her subconscious had gotten it wrong.

And it wasn't them who were getting married anyway. Dreams didn't make any sense. Her subconscious had just muddled everything up into one big mess. It was probably because she never had any closure on what had happened between them.

Maybe she should just ask him about it and find out once and for all how she'd been so wrong about how Nick had felt about her.

Marissa stretched her arms over her head and took a few deep, cleansing breaths. By the time she was on her last exhale, she felt dramatically better and had managed to calm herself down. She'd also decided that she wasn't a child anymore, and she was definitely going to confront him for an explanation about the way he'd laughed at her. No matter what the answer was, she needed to know. It was only fair.

Besides, it wasn't as if she had any real expectations about what was going on between them now. Not really. She wasn't a kid anymore. Things had changed. *She* had changed. She was no longer an insecure, lovestruck teenager.

No.

Whatever was happening—or not—with Nick, she was going in with her eyes wide open.

After a quick shower, Marissa was in their shared kitchen, pouring herself a cup of coffee, when Nick walked out of his own bedroom, looking ridiculously handsome in his workout shorts and t-shirt, and smelling even better.

"Good morning, beautiful."

Her heart soared and when he bent down to kiss her on the cheek, she thought she might totally combust.

So much for not having any expectations.

"Did you sleep well?"

She nodded, although it was a lie. "How about you? Are you ready for a day of mountain biking with Jake?" Despite Jenny's protests that they would get bruised or potentially break a leg, Jake had insisted that for the day before the wedding, he had a guys' day on the mountain trails. Jenny was still nervous about it, but Marissa was pretty sure a day at the spa would help her relax and forget about any stresses.

Marissa was also hoping it would help her.

"It should be a fun day." Nick accepted the cup of coffee she handed him with a smile and a nod and leaned against the counter. "It's been a long time since I've been on a mountain bike. I hope I remember how."

"Something tells me, you'll be just fine."

"I'm sure I will be." He winked at her and took a sip of his coffee. "And what are you doing later? Maybe we can catch up and..."

"And what?" She gave him a coy little smile, fully aware that she was flirting, and enjoying every second of it.

"And maybe have dinner?"

"Are you asking me out? Like on a date?" She held her breath and only a moment later blew it out and shook her head. "Never mind. I just remembered that it's the rehearsal dinner tonight."

"Really?"

She laughed. "Did you not read everything?"

"Seriously. There's a lot to read. These two are intense."

"They just know what they want, and there's nothing wrong with that." Marissa's smile faded. "But I guess we'll have to postpone that date."

She turned away so he wouldn't see how disappointed she must look, but he grabbed her arm and spun her around so she faced him. He grasped her by her upper arms and looked directly into her eyes. "We'll find time." He kissed her softly. "I promise."

She believed him. They chatted easily while they finished their coffee and got ready for their days. "I'll see you tonight at dinner," she said as they left their suite together.

"I'm looking forward to it." Nick gave her a kiss on the cheek this time, a move that felt very familiar and just right for that moment, because a second later, voices from down the hall interrupted them, and Nick moved a few steps away from her. She shot him a look of question, but he either didn't notice or ignored her.

They were joined by Marissa's mother and father and the moment for intimacy between them, or whatever it was that was happening, was gone as they all walked down to the lobby together. It wasn't until later, when Marissa was alone with the women, that she realized she'd completely forgotten to talk to Nick about their past.

∾

NICK WAS VERY MUCH AWARE, as he was hurtling down the mountain trails on his bike, that he should be paying a lot more attention to the terrain. At the speeds they were going, any misplaced root or rock could mean a crash and a potentially broken bone or worse.

But knowing he should pay attention and actually doing so were two totally different things, because for the life of him, Nick could not concentrate on anything besides Missy and the kiss they'd shared the night before.

He knew he was playing with fire when it came to her, but he just couldn't seem to stay away from her. The right thing to do the night before would have been to deliver her dinner and leave her alone. But he couldn't do it. Especially not after stealing that kiss from her by the pond earlier.

No. There was no way he could stay away from her. Not again.

He'd backed off once, but that was because they'd been kids. Jake would have killed him if he'd gone after Missy, but things were different now.

At least he thought they were.

"Whoa! Slow down, man." Jake yelled at him as he went flying by him on the trail, almost taking him out in the process.

Nick pressed hard on the brakes and came to a skidding stop in a flurry of dirt a few feet away.

"What the hell?" Jake demanded when Nick looked back up the trail to him. "Are you totally zoned out or what? You almost hit me."

"Sorry." Nick shook his head. "I was just lost in a thought, I guess."

"A thought?" Jake got on his bike and rode down to stand beside him. "What the hell kind of thought had you so distracted that you almost killed me the day before my wedding?" He laughed and punched Nick in the shoulder.

"Women." It wasn't a complete lie.

"Ha. I knew it. Only the finer sex can distract you like that." Jake swung his leg over his bike. "Let's take a break here and sit on that rock."

Nick nodded and followed his best friend off the trail to a little outcropping of rocks that looked out over the valley.

"This is pretty incredible," Nick said as they sat down. "What a view and holy shit, you're getting married tomorrow."

"I am." Jake laughed. "And I can't wait. She's the love of my life and I couldn't be happier."

"That's good." Nick nodded. "I'm really happy for you. Jenny's great."

"She is," Jake agreed. "But you're totally deflecting from the topic at hand." He eyed Nick. "Who is the woman who has you so distracted you almost killed me?"

"I didn't almost kill you." Nick socked his buddy in the arm. "And I didn't say it was a *woman*."

"So women in general then?" Jake laughed. "Seriously, when are you going to settle down?"

"When I find the right one." *Or convince the right one to be with me*, he thought, but didn't say out loud.

"Are you telling me that you've never met someone you could picture yourself falling in love with? You must have met thousands of women traveling the way you do. Surely one of them must be the *right* one."

Nick shrugged noncommittally. "Well, there was one. A long time ago."

"Oh yeah?"

Nick nodded. "In high school." He took a deep breath. He might as well get it over with and tell Jake that he was and always had been in love with his little sister. If anything was ever going to happen with Missy, really happen, he needed to do this. And they weren't kids anymore. Jake shouldn't have any reason to object to them being together and then finally he could tell Missy how he really felt. How he'd *always* felt. "There was a—"

"High school?" Jake interrupted him and burst into laughter. "No one knows how they feel in high school. Especially when it comes to love."

"Oh, I don't know about that—"

"And really, that's a relief to hear," Jake interrupted him again. "Because I'm not going to lie to you, buddy. There was a time when I was worried you might have a thing for my sister."

Nick's gut twisted. "Missy?"

"I know." Jake shook his head. "It's ridiculous, isn't it? But it's true. Especially senior year, and then freshman year of college, I totally thought you had a thing for Marissa. I was actually going to say something about it but then it seemed to go away."

"Oh yeah? You were going to say something?"

"Totally." Jake nodded. "Because there was no way I was going to let that happen. Not in any way."

Nick thought he might be sick. "Really?"

"Hell no, Nick. You and Missy? That's ridiculous! And so wrong. You're practically related."

"But we're not."

"You might as well be," Jake continued, oblivious of the internal struggle going on with Nick. "Besides, it's never a good idea to get involved with anyone you're close to like that. Can you imagine what would have happened if you two dated?"

He could. *They could have been insanely happy and have spent the last eight years building a life together.* But he didn't say anything.

"It would have ended in disaster and then this would all be destroyed." Jake gestured between them. "It would have ruined everything."

"Not necessarily."

Jake turned and gave Nick a strange look. "Are you kidding me right now?"

"I'm not saying—"

"There's no way, Nick. Sisters and friends are off-limits. Always have been. I'm just glad I didn't have to kick your ass back then to make my point." He slapped Nick on the back and grabbed his water bottle. "But that doesn't change the fact that you still need a woman in your life. Did you meet Jenny's cousins yet?"

Thankfully, the conversation veered away from Missy and Nick as Jake started touting the features of Jenny's cousins, having obviously been prepped by Jenny herself. Nick wasn't blind; there was definitely a set-up attempt being made. Not that he had eyes for anyone but Missy. Not even close.

But now that he knew how Jake really felt, how was he ever supposed to tell him about his feelings for Missy? Nick focused on the mountain range across from them and tried to collect his thoughts. If choosing Missy meant losing Jake, he wasn't sure it was a choice he could make.

"THIS IS GOING TO FEEL AMAZING." Marissa walked next to Jenny, each with towels wrapped around them, toward the hot pools. "There's nothing like a good soak to prepare you for dressing up in a god-aw—" Marissa stopped herself before completely blowing it and insulting the bridesmaid dress Jenny had picked out.

"What were you going to say?"

They stepped closer to the edge and tossed their towels to a nearby chair. Their mothers and a few of Jenny's cousins were already soaking, but besides a small wave in their direction, no one seemed to notice their presence.

"I was just going to say..." Marissa racked her brain for some-thing that might sound believable. "That it's nice to soak before getting dressed up." It was a lame cover-up and they both knew it.

"In a god-awful dress?" There was a twinkle in her eyes that alerted Marissa. "Like your bridesmaid dress?"

"That's not what I was trying to say, Jenny. Really, I..." Maris-sa's face flushed and she tried desperately to dig herself out of the hole she'd found herself in, but Jenny was laughing. Marissa stopped, put a hand on her hip and stared at the other woman. "What's going on?"

Jenny slipped into the water, still laughing. "Marissa, you don't really think I'd make you wear that ugly dress, do you?"

She *had* thought that, but clearly that wasn't the right answer. Marissa tilted her head in question and joined Jenny in the hot water. Instantly she felt more relaxed.

"It was Jake's idea," Jenny said. "He thought it would be funny to play a little trick on you with the dress."

"So that's not my dress?"

"Oh goodness, no!" Jenny laughed again. "Your dress will be delivered to your room this morning. It should fit perfectly. The seamstress at the shop was in on the joke."

Marissa shook her head and laughed. "Jake just always has to be playing some kind of joke, even on his wedding." She tipped her head back and let the warm water wash over her. "I don't know what else you picked out, but I have to think it's better than the fluffy thing I thought I was going to wear. And I would have worn it, too."

"I know you would have," Jenny said. "And that's why I love you. You didn't even question it. Thank you. You've really been amazing with this whole wedding. It really helps."

"Anytime. I mean, not anytime. This will be the only time."

She laughed. "But anytime you need help with anything, I'm your girl."

Jenny's smile was warm and genuine and they both fell into an easy silence, enjoying the warm water for a few minutes.

"This was such a good idea." Marissa sank deeper into the hot pool. "This water feels so good."

"Isn't it amazing?" Jenny sighed next to her. "I swear, it's totally magical the way it works out your knots and stresses."

Marissa sat up. "Don't tell me you're stressed? I know most brides get all worked up before their wedding, but you have everything so organized and taken care of. There's no way you can be stressed."

Jenny laughed and tipped her head back against the ledge. "You'd be surprised," she said. "But I will say that having you and Nick around to take care of all the things you've been handling has been awesome. You two really are the best."

Marissa closed her eyes again as she sat back into the water. Nick's face immediately popped up in her mind. She smiled a little and agreed with Jenny. "He really is the best."

"*He*?"

The woman must have had radar for the slight change in Marissa's voice, because there was a splash and when Marissa opened her eyes again, Jenny stood directly in front of her, staring.

"What was that?"

"I'm not sure what you're talking about." Marissa tried to ignore her sister-in-law to be, but even when she closed her eyes again, she could feel the other woman staring at her. Finally she gave up. Marissa sat up, ran her wet hands through her hair and scooted slightly away from Jenny.

"You know exactly what I'm talking about. What's going on with Nick?"

"Nothing." She wasn't a great liar, but maybe if she stuck as closely to the truth as possible, she could get out of the conversation without actually telling Jenny anything. "We're friends."

"Friends?"

"We've always been friends," she said. "Nick is like another brother to me. Growing up, it was like if you had one, you had both. Wherever one went, the other was there. Nick was always at our family dinners and holidays. Sometimes I had a hard time remembering that he even had another family."

Sometimes. Then there were all the other times when Marissa would lay awake, fantasizing about Nick actually being part of her family because he was with her. Because they'd grown up and gotten married. The daydreams of a lovestruck little girl? Maybe. But damned if those same feelings hadn't stuck around for all these years.

Marissa swallowed hard.

"But what about now?" Jenny pushed. "That was a long time ago. You're adults now."

"He's still part of the family." Marissa laughed in an attempt to sound casual, but judging by the look on Jenny's face, she'd failed. "He is," she said again, more serious. "Nick is and always has been part of the family."

"But you have feelings for him."

Marissa's mouth opened and closed. *Did this woman have some sort of psychic abilities?* She glanced around at the other women soaking in the pool nearby. They were either lost in conversation of their own, or drifting into sleep, but no one paid any attention to Jenny and Marissa's conversation.

A million options danced through her head. She could deny it. She could laugh it off or protest, but in the end, Marissa sighed and sank deeper into the hot, therapeutic waters. "You can't say anything."

"I knew it." Jenny didn't sound righteous, though. She only smiled sadly at Marissa. "But..."

"How do you know there's a but?"

"Because if there wasn't, we'd be celebrating you and Nick and your wedding too, don't you think?"

Marissa almost choked. *Wedding?* That was a leap. A huge leap.

"I don't think so," she finally managed to say. "It was a long time ago." She couldn't be sure why she lied to Jenny, especially considering the door was wide open for her to tell the truth, but something stopped her. Suddenly, it just didn't seem like a good idea to tell her the truth.

"What do you mean?"

Marissa laughed and looked away. "When I was a kid, I had a huge crush on Nick, but it was totally ridiculous and it was a long time ago."

Jenny eyed her carefully, as if she didn't quite believe her. "When you were a kid?"

"Well," Marissa admitted, "a teenager. For a while there, I convinced myself that I was madly in love with Nick and that we were meant to be together." She couldn't help feel a pang in her chest as she spoke the words aloud. "But then I grew up and it passed."

"It did?"

Marissa nodded. "It did."

Jenny opened her mouth to say something, but then obviously changed her mind and closed it again.

"Like I said, it was a long time ago. Nick Slater is just a friend."

"Nick Slater?" Jenny's cousin Audrey appeared beside them. "He's so hot, don't you think?"

Marissa shrugged and tried her best to swallow the jealousy that threatened to bubble over.

"Jenny told me he was single."

Audrey looked at Marissa, as she needed her clarification, so finally Marissa said, "As far as I know."

"Good." The other woman licked her lips. "I'm totally going to go after that."

"Go after that?"

"Totally. He's single—I'm single. It's a wedding. And everyone knows what happens at weddings."

Marissa was pretty sure she didn't want to know, but she couldn't help but ask, "And what's that?"

"Love connections, obviously."

"Obviously." Marissa's voice sounded numb and far away even to her own ears.

"I may have encouraged Audrey when it comes to Nick," Jenny said next to her. "After all, they are both single. But then, after the other day, I wasn't sure it was a good idea anymore."

"What?"

"Why?"

Marissa and Audrey spoke at the same time.

"Why wouldn't you think it was a good idea?" Marissa asked.

"I don't know." Jenny stretched her arms over her head and rolled her neck. "But when I saw you guys together, I just thought that maybe...but I guess it's nothing. I was wrong."

"What did you think?" Marissa's stomach flipped a little.

"I must have just seen the connection that you guys had from years ago," Jenny continued. "Because if you say there's nothing between you two, then I believe you."

She couldn't see Jenny's face, but something told Marissa that her sister-in-law to-be did not believe her.

"And I guess there's nothing stopping Audrey from *going after that.*"

"Ha!" Audrey did a shimmy in the water. "You better believe it."

The conversation around her faded away from any mention of Nick as Jenny's cousins grilled her on plans for the honeymoon. Soon, their mothers joined in and moments later, they were all whisked away by the spa staff for their various treatments.

Marissa was scheduled for a massage, but despite the masseuse's best attempts, she simply couldn't relax. Her thoughts were consumed with Nick and Jenny's cousin and what had stopped her from telling Jenny the truth.

7

"So you'll stand here, Nick." Eva, the wedding coordinator, jabbed her finger toward a spot next to the pond. They'd been at the ceremony venue for at least twenty minutes and so far, Nick had counted at least three places where he'd been told to stand.

But he didn't say anything. Instead, he dutifully smiled and nodded at the wedding coordinator and moved to the new spot.

"Great," Eva said. "I think that's much better, don't you, Jenny?"

"Absolutely. I really want the water in the background of our vows."

"Of course. But not too close to the waterfall or your guests in the back won't be able to hear you speak."

Nick stopped listening. The two women had been discussing the various pros and cons for different locations for the vows. As far as Nick could tell, they were all the same with only the slightest modifications in where he stood.

And Missy.

He looked across the space to where Missy stood, looking equally checked out and lost in thought. She looked beautiful.

He didn't think it was possible for her to look prettier than she had that morning in the kitchen handing him a cup of coffee, but it was.

She wore a simple sundress and held a single daisy in lieu of the bouquet she'd likely be holding at the actual wedding. Her hair fell around her shoulders, soft and shiny, making him want to run his fingers through it. Her skin glowed, and her lips were a pale pink. And even from a distance, he could see the way they glistened with the barest shine that called to him to kiss them.

"Hey." Jake elbowed him in the ribs and immediately guilt flooded through him.

Did Jake know what he was thinking?

Could he see the way he was looking at his little sister?

Nick turned and raised his eyebrows in response.

"Is this nuts?" Jake asked.

"Is what nuts?"

Jake sighed. "All of this. I mean, how hard can it be? I just want to be done with this already and get married."

"You are getting married."

"I know. But I'm ready now. I don't see why we need to rehearse it. Let's just do it."

Nick patted his buddy on the arm. "Patience, brother. It's going to be perfect."

"I know." He rolled his eyes. "But frankly, I think it would be perfect if we got married in a backyard somewhere. As long as I get to be with Jenny, I don't care how it happens."

Nick laughed and Missy glanced in their direction. She lifted her eyebrows in question, and Nick winked at her.

"What the hell was that?" Jake smacked him and across the aisle Missy laughed. "Did you just wink at my sister?"

Caught out, Nick brushed it off with a chuckle. "No way," he said as he avoided her eyes. "I'm just so caught up in the love here I think I got something in my eye."

"Right." Jake joined him in a laugh and when he was suffi-ciently distracted, Nick finally risked a glance back in Missy's direction. Her pretty mouth had dipped into a slight frown, her brow wrinkled in thought. And she wouldn't look at him.

SHE TRIED NOT to let it bother her, but Marissa kept replaying the scene outside in her head long after the rehearsal was finished and they'd moved inside for drinks before dinner.

He'd winked at her. She'd caught him watching her, and it had made her feel all warm inside. And then he'd winked.

But that's when the warmth faded, because a moment later Jake and Nick had obviously turned it into some kind of joke, and she'd heard him deny it.

Why?

Because she was still Missy. He still thought of her only as his best friend's little sister.

And isn't that why she'd hesitated telling Jenny the truth earlier? Because she was still so uncertain? Or because she already knew that no matter how things had changed, they would never really change?

"Hey kiddo." Her dad joined her at the bar where she'd been watching the business of the room from afar. "What are you doing hiding over here?"

She leaned into his hug. "I just needed a little break," she said. "It's already been such a busy weekend."

"That it has." He took a sip of his Scotch. "That it has."

"But it's so great for Jake," Marissa added quickly. "I mean, Jenny is great and this wedding is just going to be perfect. Really, it's been so perfect already and—"

"I know what you mean, kiddo." With his arm still around

her shoulder, he gave her a little squeeze. "You don't have to worry about me. I understand."

She laughed a little.

"Just promise me when you get married, you'll elope."

Shocked, she pulled back and stared at her dad.

"I'm joking, kiddo." He laughed. "I wouldn't miss your wedding for the world."

She shook her head, but suddenly didn't feel like smiling. "Well, you don't have to worry about that anytime soon."

Her dad tilted his head in question. "Still no one special?"

She couldn't help it. Her gaze traveled across the room to where Jenny's cousins stood around Nick, transfixed by some story he was telling. "Not really."

"I see."

"No!" She turned to her dad. "It's not like that. Really, Dad. It's not...I'm not..."

He chuckled and patted her hand. "Don't worry, kiddo. Your time will come." He kissed her on the forehead and moved away before she could say anything else. With a sigh, Marissa turned her back to the room and her life and caught the bartender's eye. "A vodka soda, please."

"Make it two."

She stiffened at the sound of Nick's voice, but then relaxed when he brushed up against her arm.

"How did you manage to tear yourself away from your admirers?" She accepted the drink from the bartender and lifted it in thanks as Nick paid for them both. "It looked like a pretty intense conversation."

"Not really." Together they turned to face the room, although neither of them were paying any attention to anything else. "I told them I had important bridal party business to attend to."

Marissa couldn't help but feel a flicker of disappointment

that he hadn't just told them that he wanted to talk to her. *Why did they have to be a secret?*

"Well, I guess that's probably true," she said after a moment. "Do we need to talk about the speeches or anything?"

Nick half turned so he faced her. "I just said that, Missy. But I really just wanted to come talk to you. I haven't seen you all day."

"Hi." She refused to look at him.

"Hi," he repeated. "How was your day at the spa?"

Marissa eyed him from the corner of her eye but still wouldn't face him. "Really?"

"Really. I want to know."

"No you don't." She shook her head and looked away.

"Missy." He grabbed her arm and forced her to look at him. "What's going on?" His touch made her all warm inside, but as soon as her eyes met his, he dropped his hand. She shook her head and looked away. "Seriously," Nick said. "What's going on? This morning you were all—"

"I was what?" She hissed beneath her breath. "I was all into you? Is that what you were going to say?"

"Well...no...but..." He glanced around to see whether anyone was watching. "Keep your voice down, or—"

"Or everyone will hear?" She put her hands on her hips. Enough was enough. Whatever *had* happened between them obviously wasn't anything important. Not to him anyway. Eight years ago, he'd laughed at her. This time, he'd treated her like a dirty little secret.

Either way, it wasn't good enough.

"I don't care if anyone hears, Nick. But obviously you do." Her voice shook and she hated it, but she still needed to say everything she was thinking. She had to get it out this time. She could no longer keep it inside. "Because the truth is—"

"No," he interrupted her. "Not here." He grabbed her hand

and pulled her away from the bar and out a side door that led to a pathway that snaked around the building and into the surrounding woods. "Whatever you have to say to me, do it out here."

"Because God forbid you're seen talking with me in public. Right, Nick?"

"No." He frowned. "That's not what this is about at all, Missy. Just stop."

But she couldn't stop. She'd had enough and she was hurt and it was all too much.

"No, Nick. I just—"

"Missy," he said again. "Stop. Please."

She took a breath. And then another.

"This is Jake and Jenny's weekend," Nick continued. "I just didn't want this to impact their weekend in any way or draw attention away from them."

That was a good point.

Marissa swallowed hard. "Right."

"Now what were you going to say to me?"

8

*N*ick managed to calm her down enough that she no longer looked as though she was going to spit nails at him, but it still wasn't enough.

Or maybe it was.

"I can't do this, Nick."

His heart sank because he knew what she was saying. Without her even having to speak the words out loud, he knew what she meant. But then she clarified.

"Eight years ago, I was in love with you." Her words hit him so hard his heart fluttered. "I thought you loved me too."

Desperately, every part of him wanted to tell her how much he had loved her. How much he *still* loved her. Had never *stopped* loving her. He opened his mouth but closed it again when he couldn't find the words.

"I took a chance, Nick." She looked so vulnerable in front of him, pouring her heart out and opening herself to what had to be the most sensitive part of her, but still, he was frozen, unable to appropriately respond. "And you laughed. You actually *laughed.*"

The word was like daggers in his gut. He flinched, although

it was doubtful she noticed. He should have said a million things. He could have come up with a million ways to defend or explain his actions of that night eight years ago, but he couldn't. It was his chance to tell her why he'd turned her away. Why he'd *pushed* her away that night. How it saved both of them and the family they both loved.

But he couldn't.

He was a coward.

Nick's mouth opened and closed and still, no words came out. Not the ones that mattered, anyway. The only thing he could say was, "I don't remember that."

It was a lie. An ugly, hurtful lie and judging by the look on her face, it was a lie that cut her to the quick. It hurt him physically to watch the pain it caused her to digest that lie. Because the truth was, he remembered that night in vivid Technicolor.

Of course he did.

He remembered the way she'd come to him. Heady and excited on the high of graduating high school, with her whole life in front of her.

She'd looked amazing.

And she walked right up to him, told him how much she loved him, and kissed him. Just like that.

It was the single best kiss of his life.

Hands down.

Until last night.

But instead of doing what he should have done—instead of wrapping his arms around her and holding her close while he pressed his lips to hers the way he'd wanted to for at least over a year—he'd pushed her away. And then he'd laughed.

It was the only thing he knew to do because eight years ago, Jake had taken Nick aside and told him how much he valued their relationship. How much their *brotherhood* meant to him. Maybe he knew what Nick was thinking when it came to his sister. Maybe he didn't. But either way, Jake had hugged him and told him how nothing could ever come between them. Not even a girl. *Especially* not a girl. And not even an hour after that conversation, Missy had come home from her graduation dance and kissed him.

He'd panicked.

How could he sacrifice his entire relationship with Jake—his *family*—for a girl?

Not even for Missy.

And eight years later, it was the same thing all over again. His relationship with Jake meant the world. The Duncans were everything to him. More family than his own. Heck, after this weekend, he probably didn't even have a job with his family business and his own father would have even less of a reason to talk to him on a monthly basis. No. Jake and the Duncans were everything to him.

But this is different.

"You don't remember?" Missy took a step back, the hurt lining her face. "Really? You don't remember the way I told you how I'd loved you for years?"

Stunned, he stood in front of her, dumbfounded.

"I kissed you, Nick."

Still, he said nothing.

"And you kissed me back."

He shook his head slightly.

"You did." Her words were almost a cry. "And then you pushed me away and laughed at me."

Nick struggled not to react to her words. He struggled not to reach for her and apologize and kiss away the pain those actions caused her so long ago. The actions he'd regretted for years. He wanted to do all of those things more than anything else in his life, but Jake's words from earlier that day rang in his ears again.

It would have ruined everything. So instead he said, "Missy, I'm sorry if you ever thought our relationship was—"

"Stop." Missy shook her head and took a distancing step backward. "Whatever you're going to say, don't. Whatever excuse you're going to make, stop. I don't want to hear it." She put her hands on her ears like a child and stepped farther back into the wooded path. "I can't hear it."

"Missy."

"No." She shook her head. "I just can't, Nick." She turned away from him, and said the last words before she turned and fled into the trees. "Not again."

As MUCH AS she wanted to, Marissa couldn't stay away from the rehearsal dinner all night. She owed it to Jenny to be a good maid of honor—the best one, really. And that definitely included being at her side for the rehearsal despite the fact that her heart was completely shattered and she felt like the world's biggest idiot.

She should have seen it coming. She sort of *had* seen it coming, really. Well, her subconscious had, anyway, with that dream.

But it was just a dream and this was real life and Nick Slater had broken her heart for the second time and she'd let him.

I thought this time was different.

Despite everything, the voice inside her continued to try to make sense of what had happened. But there was no sense to it.

In the cool evening air, Marissa took a deep breath and then another, trying desperately to clear her head. She needed to pull herself together before going back in there. It would almost be time for dinner and, unlike the first time Nick had embarrassed her and hurt her, she couldn't just run away and avoid him for another eight years.

Besides, she was a bigger person than that. She was a strong, confident, self-assured woman. She would not let this define her.

Not again.

She made a quick stop in the restroom to splash water on her face and smooth her hair back before she headed back into the restaurant. It was perfect timing, as everyone was just finding their way to their seats. She did a quick scan around the room, and saw Nick in a corner, alone. He held a glass of what looked to be whiskey.

She looked away and went to find her seat.

Fortunately, there was an empty seat next to her mother. There didn't seem to be place settings this time, so she slid into the spot and picked up her menu, pretending to be engrossed in the pasta options so she wouldn't have to make conversation.

"Where've you been, honey?"

Clearly her mother wasn't picking up on her *I don't want to talk* vibes.

"I just went for a walk."

"But it's dark."

Marissa nodded. "It is. I didn't go far."

"There are bears out there, Marissa." She didn't even have to look to know her mother's face would be screwed up in worry and wrinkled in intense concern. If there was one thing her mother did well, it was worry. "And cougars. Marissa, we're in the mountains. That was reckless."

With a sigh, she put the menu down and made eye contact. "I promise it wasn't reckless." She tried very hard to keep her voice down. She didn't want to attract any attention and if her mother continued on the way she was going, that's exactly what they were going to do. "I was only outside for a minute and I stayed on the path. You could hardly even call it a walk."

"Then why did you say it was a walk?"

Marissa sighed again and tried very hard not to get flustered. "Mom, it's fine. Really. I just needed a few minutes alone. I was perfectly safe the whole time."

"Who was safe?" Jake sat down across from them and immediately jumped into the conversation. "What's going on? Marissa, why do you look so—"

"I'm safe," she interrupted him before he could point out how terrible she looked. Because she did look terrible—how could she not? She felt even worse than she looked. "I just went for a little walk outside and Mom got her panties all in a twist about it. Nothing bad is going to happen to me at the Lodge, Mom."

Unless you counted getting your heart broken, she wanted to add, but didn't. She picked up her menu again and stared at the chicken rotini dish. She could eat it quickly and then beg off to finish her speech. Surely it was legitimate to use that excuse two nights in a row when you were the maid of honor.

Even if it wasn't. Marissa wasn't sure she cared anymore. She just wanted to get out of there. Away from Nick and his gaze that she could feel on her. Not that she would look to confirm. There was no way she was going to look at him.

She was going to hold her head up high and be strong because that was the only thing left to do.

Fortunately, her mother dropped her concern about Marissa's safety and focused instead on the proceedings of the evening, which ultimately went quite quickly and smoothly. There were a few speeches and toasts and meals were served.

Somewhere around the time the dishes were being cleared and dessert was being prepared, Marissa noticed that Nick was gone.

Jake noticed her looking in the direction of Nick's empty seat and leaned across the table. "Have you noticed that Nick's acting weird this weekend?"

"No." She shook her head quickly and looked away. "Why would you say that?"

"Because something's up," Jake mused. "I assumed it was just with work and the way he blew off his dad to be here. I mean, not that it couldn't be the reason he's acting strange, because no kidding, his job is totally on the line right now."

"That must be it."

"No," her brother said. "There's something more. He mentioned something about a woman earlier."

Marissa's ears perked up, but she tried even harder to look disinterested. "Did he?"

"Yes and no." Jake took a sip of his drink before he turned his attention back to his sister. "He actually started to tell me about a girl he thought he loved way back in high school."

Marissa almost spat out her drink.

"I told him it was crazy," Jake said. "No one knows what they want in high school. Can you even imagine if you had to marry the one you thought you loved back then?"

She could imagine it. That was the whole problem.

9

"*I* really can't deal with this right now, Dad." Nick glanced at his watch. He was already late. He'd promised Jake he'd be in his room by ten to help him get ready for the wedding. And of course to calm his nerves. So far, he was failing his duties as his best man. But only because he'd made the mistake of answering his cell phone when it rang.

"You *will* deal with this right now, Nick," his dad roared through the line. "This is my company and I will not have you treating it like a passing interest."

"I'm not, Dad." Nick put his dad on speakerphone while he moved around the room, gathering his things. "I told you, I'll get on the plane first thing on Monday."

"You'll get on the plane tonight, son. You're needed in meetings on Monday."

"No." He shook his head. His dad never was one for emotions of any kind and he didn't have any friends to speak of, so Nick hadn't been surprised when he didn't understand that Nick had to be present for Jake's wedding. "My best friend is getting married, Dad. I can't miss it."

"Leave after the ceremony," he said after a moment. "You can be in the city by seven and get on the eight o'clock flight."

"No, Dad. It's not—"

"It's not an option, son. Get on the plane or I will find a new international affairs advisor."

Nick froze. His father didn't make idle threats. "Dad, that's not fair. I've done everything for this company."

"Not everything. You're not in China."

"I will be." He picked up the phone and held it close to his mouth. "I cannot miss this wedding. It's Jake. I'll get on the flight on—"

"Tonight, Nick. It's not negotiable."

Nick opened his mouth to argue again, but his father had already hung up. "Dammit." He threw the phone across the room and let it crash against the wall. Growing up, Nick thought his father to be cold and uncaring, but he hadn't realized the scope of his father's drive to succeed at all costs. Not until he'd started working for him. For the last few years, it hadn't bothered him because Nick had largely ignored his father, as much as he could, anyway. But now...he had no choice.

There was no way he could ignore an ultimatum like that. Jake would understand. He would be there for the ceremony. That was the most important part, right? And the pictures...he could probably sneak in a few pictures before leaving. It was a two-hour drive back to the city and that would put him at the airport at six. It would be tight. But he could do it.

"Dammit." He picked up his phone and shoved it in his pocket before he grabbed up his tux and rushed out of the room. He knew Missy wasn't there. He'd heard her door open and shut hours earlier. And as much as he wanted to go out and talk to her about everything that had happened at the rehearsal dinner, he hadn't.

The truth was, he didn't know what to say. He didn't know

how to tell her about his feelings for her and how he'd been in love with her since they were kids. He didn't know how to say any of that and then not pull her into his arms and never let go.

But he'd have to, because...Jake. *How could he jeopardize everything?*

Nick glanced in the direction of Missy's room as he passed through their suite. It wouldn't be an issue soon enough. He'd stick around for the wedding and then get out of there. And spend the next eight years trying to forget her.

Again.

Maybe this time it would actually work.

MARISSA HAD SPENT the better part of the day primping and fussing. Mostly over the bride, but also a little bit on herself, too. Jenny was right: the dress she'd picked out for her, the *real* dress, was gorgeous and she felt beautiful in it. It was a soft coral, made with a soft, flowy fabric that hugged her bodice before falling into a light, airy skirt that flirted with her knees. It was too bad she wasn't in the mood to be dressed up, have her hair done, or really...anything.

All Marissa really wanted to do was crawl into her bed and feel sorry for herself, not that it was an option. Especially not with the music starting and the time almost upon them.

"Are you ready?" Eva, the wedding planner, tapped her on the shoulder.

Marissa almost jumped. She managed a smile and a nod. "I'm ready." She turned to Jenny, who looked stunning in her creamy lace gown. Her hair was twisted up in a simple knot with a few flowers tucked in that matched the bouquet of wildflowers in her hands. She looked like a princess.

"Jenny?" Marissa asked. "How are you doing?"

Her soon-to-be sister-in-law smiled broadly. "I've never been better."

"And you look amazing." Her father appeared at her side and kissed her cheek. "Is everyone ready to do this? You can change your mind, you know?" He was kidding, but Jenny shook her head.

"Never in a million years," she said.

"Okay." Eva grabbed Marissa's hand. "That's your cue." She led her toward the door. "Remember. Walk slow, in time with the music. When you get to the altar, you can give your brother a little hug or whatever feels natural and then quickly take your place."

Marissa nodded and stepped through the door.

The moment she started her walk down the aisle, everyone turned and all eyes were on her. But there was only one set of eyes she was worried about.

Nick was watching her. She could feel it, but she refused to look. They hadn't spoken at all last night, nor this morning. In fact, the last time they exchanged words was when she'd lost her temper and told him exactly how she felt.

It was mortifying.

But she couldn't think of that right now. She could only think about keeping the smile on her face and holding it together long enough for Jake and Jenny to get married. Then she could fall apart.

Somehow, she reached the altar and moved in to give her big brother a hug. She squeezed her eyes shut and whispered in his ear. "I'm so proud of you, Jake. Jenny is amazing."

"Thanks, sis. That means a lot." *Was it her imagination or did her brother sound choked up?* She opened her eyes to check, but instead of seeing Jake, she looked directly into Nick's eyes.

He smiled at her and she froze.

"You look beautiful." He mouthed the words, but she could hear them as if he'd yelled them at her.

She hesitated a moment longer before Jake took a step back and she remembered that she was supposed to take her place.

Quickly, she looked away and went to stand on the other side of the altar. Marissa could feel Nick's eyes on her, but she purposely kept them averted, focusing instead on the door where Jenny would be appearing.

Seconds later, a gasp went up from the crowd when Jenny stepped out of the door with her father.

She was even more stunning than she'd been a moment ago. A quick glance at her brother confirmed that Jake was thinking the same thing. His bride was gorgeous.

The rest of the ceremony passed in a blur as the happy couple exchanged their vows next to the little pond in the courtyard where only a few days earlier, she and Nick had exchanged a kiss.

It wasn't real. She had to continually remind herself that there was nothing real between them. There hadn't been eight years ago, and there wasn't now.

Finally, the music started for the procession. Jenny and Jake waved their hands in the air to whoops and hollers from the crowd and danced down the aisle. A second later, Marissa was jolted out of her trance by the hot touch of Nick's hand on her bare skin.

She yanked it away before she realized they were meant to walk down the aisle together.

"Missy," he whispered under his breath. "We have to go."

She nodded and allowed him to take her hand. Somehow she managed a smile despite the intense feelings crashing through her just from the touch of Nick's skin on hers. Thankfully, Nick was in control as they did their own little dance and celebration down the aisle and around the corner, out of sight from the guests.

The moment it was safe, she yanked her hand away from him and wrapped it tightly around her bouquet.

"Missy, I—" Nick tried to grab her hand back, but she turned and gave Jake and Jenny a big hug.

"Congratulations, you two! I'm so happy for you." She didn't even have to fake the smile as she congratulated her brother and new sister-in-law. There was no couple in the entire world she could be happier for.

"Me too." Nick's arms were around her as he encompassed them all in a bear hug. She couldn't help it, she stiffened, but determined not to make a scene, forced herself to relax. "It was a beautiful wedding, man," Nick was saying. "I couldn't be happier for you guys."

"It's not over yet," Jake said as the hug mercifully broke up. "Tonight is when the real celebrating happens. And I can't wait to see your dance that you two have been working on."

The dance. She'd forgotten all about the dance. There was no way. She couldn't. Marissa started to shake her head, but Jake stopped her.

"I bet you thought that the dance was a practical joke, just like the bridesmaid dress?"

"Only you would think of pranking me on *your* wedding day, big brother."

"Maybe," he said. "But the dance isn't a prank."

"What?"

"It's not," Jenny chimed in. "I really think it'll be awesome to see you two do the dance. And when Jake told me it was your favorite movie, well...I can't wait to see what you two have come up with."

She shook her head again and backed up. Directly into Nick, whose hands came up to her shoulders. She couldn't make a scene, but the touch of him on her bare skin was almost more than she could handle.

"About the dance," Nick said. "Jake, I need to talk to you for a minute."

IT WASN'T the best time, but he needed to tell Jake he had to leave. That he needed to acquiesce to his father and get on a flight to China, even if it was his best friend's wedding. However, the moment he had his best friend's attention, with his new bride at his side, and Missy standing there with his hands on her soft, delicate shoulders, he couldn't do it.

"What about the dance?"

He opened his mouth to tell him he was leaving.

Missy turned and looked at him, a question in her eyes. It stopped him.

Jake would understand if he left. Heck, Jenny would understand, too. But Missy...if he left now, it would be over. Any chance he might have to fix things or see where they could go would be gone. He'd walked away once, leaving her crushed and his own heart battered as well.

In that instant, it was clear.

He couldn't do it again.

He wouldn't.

And even though he had no idea how he could possibly explain to his best friend that even though he'd made it perfectly clear to stay away from his sister...he simply couldn't. Because he was totally and completely in love with Missy and it was *way* past due that he tell her exactly how he felt...

Even though he had no idea how to do *any* of that, Nick just knew the one thing he couldn't do again—*wouldn't* do again—was break her heart.

Nick smiled, the decision made. "I just can't wait to show you our moves. We've been practicing, haven't we, Missy?"

She looked as if she might cry, but she nodded instead. "We have," she agreed. "And I think you're going to be impressed."

Nick gave her shoulders a squeeze, wishing desperately he could just pull her into his arms right there and kiss away all the pain he'd seen in her eyes, and the hurt—that despite her best efforts—was all over her face for anyone to see if they weren't too busy looking at the happy couple.

But it wasn't the right time.

Not yet.

"Well, I can't wait," Jenny said moments before their quiet moment was over. The blonde, loud, and totally in control wedding planner appeared and directed them all toward the photographer. Reluctantly, Nick released Missy's shoulders and walked in the direction they'd been ordered to go, following behind the women.

Jake grabbed his arm and pulled him back. "Did you need to tell me something, man?"

Nick shook his head.

"It seemed like you might have something to say. Don't tell me your dad called and—"

"No way." His best friend knew him too well. "It's nothing," Nick said. "And don't worry about my dad, or China, or anything else. I wouldn't miss tonight for anything."

"Good." Jake slapped him on the back. "I'm really glad you're here, man. You're my brother."

Nick nodded. *His brother.*

Hopefully he'd still feel that way by the end of the night.

10

"It was a beautiful ceremony, wasn't it?" Marissa's Aunt Caroline greeted her at the reception with a hug and a smile. They had a few minutes after the photos to grab a drink, before the bride and groom were announced and the reception would start. It had been a busy day, and Marissa was looking forward to a quick glass of wine before her speech, but she hadn't even made it to the bar before getting stopped by her family. "I just can't believe little Jakey is all grown up and got married. I remember when you two were just running around naked in the sprinkler."

Marissa laughed. "I know it's hard to believe," she said. "And it really was such a perfect day."

"And you look gorgeous, dear." Aunt Caroline squeezed her hand. "Maybe soon it will be your wedding we're attending?"

Marissa forced a smile. It hadn't been the first comment from her extended family. "Maybe someday," she said. "I really should be—"

"Oh, Marissa, you have to meet Bert Wallace's boy." Her aunt started to drag her away from the bar and in the direction of a group of people, presumably one of them Bert Wallace's boy, whoever that was. "I think he'll be just perfect for you. Maybe it will be a match."

"Oh, Aunt Caroline, I really—"

"Nonsense," she interrupted. "You need to put yourself out there if you're ever going to—"

"There you are." Nick's voice saved her, followed by his hand on her back, a touch that sent heat racing through her. "I've been looking everywhere for you." Gently, he pulled Marissa away from her aunt and when she turned to give him a grateful look, he placed a glass of white wine in her hand. "I thought you could use this."

Grateful, Marissa took the glass and immediately took a sip.

"I'm so sorry," Nick said to her aunt, "but I really need to borrow Marissa."

She shrugged apologetically. "The duties of a maid of honor are never done."

"Absolutely. You go, dear. We'll catch up later."

Marissa gave her aunt a quick kiss on the cheek. "Of course."

"And don't forget about Bert Wallace's boy."

"I...ummm..."

"We really should get going." Nick gently steered her away.

When they were a safe distance away, Nick leaned down to whisper in her ear. "You're welcome."

"For what exactly?"

"Saving you, of course."

Despite herself, she laughed.

"And don't worry," he added. "I'll make sure to personally deliver you to Bert Wallace's boy."

She smacked his arm. "You wouldn't."

Nick stopped and spun her so she had no choice but to look at him. "Only if you wanted to," he said with sincerity. "I just want you to be happy."

She could see there was so much more that he wasn't saying.

But before either of them could say anything, the lights blinked, which was their cue. The bride and groom would be ready to enter the reception anytime, which meant their rest time was over. They both still had more duties to attend to, including delivering their speeches, and of course, the dance.

"We should go." Marissa pulled away and adjusted her dress.

"Wait." He reached out to stop her and Marissa turned.

She was immediately struck by how hard it was to look him in the eye. It hurt her heart to look at him and know that somehow she needed to be able to move past whatever feelings she had or thought she had for him.

It was time.

"We have to go," she said again, and turned quickly to slip from his grasp.

HE SHOULD HAVE TOLD her right then and there how he felt about her, but he couldn't find the words. And finally when he thought maybe he could just say it, it was too late and she was gone.

The day had completely gotten away from him, but there was no way he was going to let the night end without knowing one way or another whether she felt the same way that he did.

He'd given up his career for her, not that it mattered. It had taken him way too long to realize it, but Nick knew with no uncertainty that he would give anything for Missy. Anything at all. And he was going to tell her that, too.

But first he needed to find the right time.

He managed to focus on the wedding long enough to clap and cheer and raise a glass in toast at the appropriate times, and then finally it was his turn to get up and say a few words.

Nick was no stranger to public speaking. In fact, his job

required him to make presentations almost weekly. At least it used to. Whether he had a job to go back to or not wasn't the point and he couldn't worry about it. Not when he needed to focus on making the best speech of his life.

Jake deserved it.

He walked slowly up to the podium, taking the time to compose himself and gather his thoughts. Speaking in front of large crowds might be old hat, but that didn't mean he was any less nervous.

Because all of his corporate presentations lacked one thing.

Missy.

He didn't even have to look to know she was watching him closely. He could feel her eyes on him and that made him nervous as hell.

Nick cleared his throat and tapped the microphone, a move he immediately regretted as the speakers squealed in protest. There were a few snickers around the room but he ignored them. He pulled a folded piece of paper from his suit jacket, unfolded it carefully and looked up.

Right at Missy.

He smiled and forced himself to focus on the matter at hand.

"Good evening," he started. "Today I had the great pleasure of standing next to this man while he married the love of his life. And let me tell you, it *was* a pleasure to watch, because there were times when I wasn't sure this day would *ever* come."

That comment brought laughter, and he knew he had the crowd. After a few more jokes about Jake, it was time for Nick to get down to business.

"With all seriousness though," he said, and waited for the room to recover from his last story about the two of them in high school. "I really did hope this day would come for Jake, because even though I'm the one standing up here as the best man, it's Jake who truly is the best man I know. It's been my privilege over the years to grow up with him, get in trouble with him, and watch him turn into one of the strongest, most successful men I know, with the kindest heart." There were a few *aw*'s from around the room. Nick turned to look at his best friend and continued. "I've never been able to define our relationship with the simple word of *friend*. It just doesn't seem like enough to describe what we share together. You've always been more of a brother and I'm proud to call you that." Nick turned to Jenny. "It was always going to take a special woman to be worthy of my brother, and I knew the moment he introduced me to you, Jenny. You were it. Not only are you beautiful, smart, kind and loving—you can put up with him."

More laughter.

"Seriously. You two are amazing and I wish you all the love and happiness this life has to offer you. It's my hope that one day..." Nick's eyes locked with Missy's. He caught himself before it became obvious that he'd gotten lost in her and cleared his throat before he continued. "That one day I'll experience the same," he managed to finish. "If you'll join me in raising a glass to the happy couple. To Jake and Jenny."

"To Jake and Jenny!" everyone chorused. But Nick didn't notice because he was too busy watching Missy, who was staring at him. She smiled when she caught him looking. But it didn't reach her eyes and that killed him.

AFTER NICK, it was Marissa's turn. She didn't know Jenny nearly as well as Nick and Jake knew each other, so there were far fewer personal stories, but the sentiment was the same and when Marissa raised a glass in a toast to her new sister, more than a few people shed a tear. Including Marissa.

The day had been an emotional one for so many reasons. And it was far from over. The hardest part was yet to come.

The dance.

She'd done a good job not thinking about it for most of the day—at least not too much—but it couldn't be avoided forever. And with the speeches over and the first dance about to start, the time was quickly approaching.

"Are you ready for this?"

Nick appeared next to her side as if he'd read her mind.

She nodded.

"We don't have to do it if you really don't want to, you know?" Marissa turned to give him an "are you completely out of your mind" look. "Okay, you're right. We have to do it," he conceded. "It is Jake and Jenny."

She turned back to where the newlyweds were walking out on the dance floor. "Exactly," she said. "And it's about them. Not us."

"It's kind of about us."

Had he really just said that?

She gave him a confused look but he only shrugged and said, "You know it is."

"I don't know that, actually."

But she did. At least a little bit. Her favorite movie had always been *Dirty Dancing* but not just because of Patrick Swayze's moves that had every teenage girl swooning. It was mostly because of the one night when she was fifteen, sick with strep throat, unable to go to the school dance, and feeling sorry for herself. She'd curled up on the couch and turned on the movie that always made her feel better when Nick had walked in. He'd come to pick up Jake to go to the dance, but he'd taken one look at her and plopped down on the couch right next to her.

Jake had gone to the dance on his own that night and despite the fact that she'd had a fever and it hurt to swallow water, Marissa had the best night of her life.

It was the night she'd officially fallen in love with Nick Slater.

But there was no way Nick could know that and there was definitely no way Jake and Jenny could know.

Could they?

But there was no time to ask Nick or say anything else because the music was starting and the happy couple started moving around the floor.

They were beautiful and the way they looked into each other's eyes brought a tear to Marissa's eye.

And then another.

It didn't take long before she couldn't stop the stream of tears rolling down her face.

"Hey." Nick put his arm around her and pulled her close. She tried not to but she inhaled his scent and leaned into his touch. *How was it that everything about Nick felt so right when it was still so wrong?* It didn't seem fair. "You're not supposed to cry." He leaned in and whispered in her ear. "It's a happy day."

"It's the happiest." Marissa wished she believed those words just a little bit more. At least as far as she was concerned. "I'm not sad." *Another lie.*

"I'm glad to hear it." He squeezed her shoulder a little more in a brotherly jostle. It was enough to jar her into reality. Because the reality was that her teenage dreams about being with Nick Slater were never going to come true. He was never going to see her as more than a little sister.

But the way he kissed her.

She shook her head and pulled away from him. The kisses didn't matter. No matter what she'd managed to tell herself, they weren't real. All she had to do was get through the dance. She only had to survive a few minutes of being close to him, letting him hold her in his arms and spin her around the dance floor. She could do it.

Marissa took a deep breath and focused on Jake and Jenny. They had practically stopped moving and were simply staring into each other's eyes, swaying to the rhythm of the music. Marissa couldn't help the little smile that tickled her lips because she knew how long Jenny and Jake had practiced their dance so it would be perfect. Another tear came to her eye when she realized that all of the practicing in the world couldn't have prepared them for that moment. The way they were looking at each other, so much love in their eyes, their dance *was* perfect.

A moment later, it was over and the DJ was back on the microphone, announcing Nick and Marissa.

Nick took a step back and extended his hand gallantly. "Missy? May I have this dance?"

She couldn't help but giggle a little as she wiped the last trace of the tear away from her eye. "You know you can."

She might as well try to enjoy herself. After all, it was Nick and they *were* at Jake's wedding. Despite everything that had happened between them—and *not* happened—there was no one else Marissa could imagine dancing with in that moment.

Her knees shook as they walked to the center of the dance floor. Nick stood behind her and reflexively she leaned back into him a little bit. When they'd rehearsed the dance a few nights earlier, they thought it would be funny if they started the dance the same way Patrick Swayze and Jennifer Grey did in the movie, so when the familiar strains of the song floated through the air, Nick lifted her arm and traced his fingers up her bare skin.

Marissa thought she might come completely undone. Fortunately, when he reached her hand, Nick clenched it tightly and spun her out quickly to a cheer from the audience.

Neither of them were talented enough dancers to replicate the entire famous dance from the movie, but they moved together easily and before long, Marissa was completely lost in the moment, in the song, the dance, and in Nick.

The song began to wind down and Nick spun her out one more time before he pulled her in tight. He wrapped his arms around her and held her close.

"Missy, I need to—"

"No." She shook her head. It had been a perfect dance. The best way she could think of to close that chapter of her life and move on. "Please don't say anything. We're dancing."

He didn't loosen his grip. "I need to tell you—"

"Let's hear it for the gorgeous maid of honor and the best man!" The DJ's announcement caused the distraction she needed and Marissa slipped out of Nick's arms just as the dance floor began to fill up with wedding guests who were more than ready to get the party started.

The party might only just be getting started, but the last thing Marissa felt like doing was celebrating.

11

"*Y*ou looked great out there." Audrey had managed to corner Nick when he'd tried to go looking for Missy. "You're quite the dancer."

"Thank you." He tried to look around Audrey's shoulder, without appearing too rude, but he needed to find Missy. Holding her in his arms on the dance floor had felt so right, as if his body had been made to be with hers.

He needed to tell her how he felt. And he hoped like hell it wasn't too late.

"Maybe we could share a dance this evening?" She batted her eyelashes and popped her hip out to the side.

It's not that she wasn't an attractive woman. She was.

But she wasn't Missy.

Damn. It had always been Missy. It always would be.

"Maybe," he said hesitantly. "But I really do have to..." He spotted her. She was seated at a table with her parents and a few other relatives. She was nodding at something someone was saying, but the smile he so loved to see on her beautiful face was nowhere in sight.

He needed to change that.

"Would you excuse me?" Without waiting for a response, he slipped away and made his way first toward the DJ booth. With the party just getting started, Nick knew it wouldn't be an easy sell, but he was prepared to do whatever it took. As it turned out, it only took a twenty dollar bill and a quick explanation as to what he was trying to do in order to have his request heard.

Next, with his eyes locked on his target, Nick walked directly to the table where the family he'd always thought of as his own was sitting. What he was about to do could potentially destroy everything, but it was a risk he had to take.

"Excuse me." He interrupted the conversation. "I'm sorry to interrupt."

"Nick." Alan stood and grabbed an empty chair, dragging it over. "Sit with us. Your speech was excellent."

He ignored the extra chair and continued to stand.

"It really was," Patrice chimed in. "What a lovely tribute to your relationship with Jake. You two really are like brothers. Always have been."

Nick swallowed hard, but the lump in his throat wouldn't budge.

"You should know, Nick," Alan said. "We've always thought of you like another son."

He again attempted to swallow before abandoning the idea. "Thank you," he said instead. "You all are so very important to me as well." His gaze landed on Missy. She blushed, and something that looked like pain crossed her face.

He knew he'd hurt her.

He hated it. He'd never do it again.

He just had to make her hear him.

Alan was saying something else, but Nick didn't hear it, because all the noise in the room faded away as he looked at Missy and the first few notes of the song he'd requested started to play. "Missy? Would you dance with me?" He held out a hand and hoped she wouldn't see the way it shook.

"We already danced." It was an immediate response, but Nick could see the exact moment she realized what song was playing. "Hungry Eyes," the second most iconic song from the movie *Dirty Dancing*. And Missy's actual favorite. She shook her head and tried to look away, but his words stopped her.

"This one is for us, Missy."

She turned back and looked straight into his eyes. Nick could see the confusion and indecision warring on her beautiful face. It may only have taken a few seconds, but it felt like an eternity before she finally nodded and took his hand. "Okay."

He was vaguely aware of her family watching them as he led her to the dance floor and immediately spun her into his arms, but he didn't care because he would risk everything if it meant having a chance to finally realize the love he'd felt for so long.

Missy allowed him to move her easily around the dance floor for a few beats before she said, "You requested this song?"

"Of course."

Her gorgeous eyes filled with tears and it broke his heart. "Why?" she asked. "Why would you do that?"

"Because it's your favorite."

She looked up at him as a tear rolled down her cheek.

"I know Jake thought he was being funny with his song choice for our dance, but I know this was your favorite song from that movie. I remembered."

"You did. Why?"

He pulled her close and turned them gently in time to the music. "Because I've remembered everything, Missy." She looked down, but he tilted her chin up with two fingers. "Everything."

"Nick, don't do this."

"I have to."

She shook her head and tried to pull away, but Nick held her tighter. "I do," he said. "Because I should have done it years ago."

"Nick, I can't do this again."

The look on her face was almost too much for him. *Was it too late? Had he really missed his chance with her?* He refused to believe it.

"I'm just starting to—"

"No." He stopped moving and with one hand still on her waist, he moved the other to her cheek. "Whatever it is you don't want to do again, don't worry. Please. I'm not going to hurt you, Missy."

"But you are." Her voice was somewhere between a laugh and a cry. "You said it yourself. You're like family. We're family. My brother thinks of you like a brother. My mom and dad think of you like a son, and—"

"And you?"

"What?"

"How do you think of me?"

"Nick."

He knew how he thought of her. He'd known since he was sixteen. And it had only been concreted the moment she kissed him and he'd made the biggest mistake of his life. It wouldn't happen again.

"Missy." He lifted both hands and cupped her face right there in the middle of the dance floor because it didn't matter who saw them. It no longer mattered whether anyone was paying attention to them or had any opinion of what they were doing. Because the only thing that mattered was the amazing woman in front of him and the realization that he would do anything to keep her from getting away from him again. "You want to know how I think of you?"

She nodded and Nick didn't hesitate.

"I think of you first thing in the morning. Before my eyes

even open and I haven't yet had a chance to realize I'm awake. I think of you while I sip my coffee, wondering if you're having some too. With just a splash of water in the first cup, just the way you like it. I think of you all through the day, sometimes so much so that I can't get my work done because all I can think about is what you're doing. I think about you right before I fall asleep, wishing you were with me, laying in my arms. I think of you in my dreams. Every single night. All night." He used his thumb to wipe a stray tear that had slipped down her cheek. "Marissa Duncan, I can't even put into words what I think of you because you're *all* I think about. And you're all I think about, because I'm desperately, madly in love with you."

She didn't say anything, and she probably would have tried to take a step back if Nick hadn't been holding her firmly. She shook her head. Just a little. But Nick noticed.

"No," he said. "Don't do that. Don't dismiss this. I meant every word I said."

"You...you called me Marissa."

HE'D CALLED HER MARISSA. That was the one thing out of everything he'd said that she could focus on.

It seemed the safest.

But he'd said other things too.

He'd said he loved her.

He'd said he loved her.

He loved *her.*

Her head spun and she couldn't focus on anything. For a moment, she thought she might fall over, but Nick's arms were there, holding her up. *Nick. He was there.*

And he loved her.

She looked up at him. "You called me Marissa," she said again.

Nick laughed. "It seemed like the right time." His hand cupped her cheek and she leaned into the touch. "Did you hear everything else I said?"

She nodded.

"I mean it. I love you."

The words hit her in the heart and finally they registered.

"You love me."

"I always have," he said. "I was too young, stupid, and scared eight years ago to tell you then and I lived with the regret of that every day since. I thought I'd one day get over it and get over you, but I never did. Not really. And when I saw you in the restaurant the other night, I finally realized what my heart had always known."

"But you..." Her instinct was to turn away and run from what was happening, but that was only because she wasn't really sure what was happening. She'd dreamed of the moment that Nick would hold her in his arms and finally tell her he loved her. But she wasn't quite ready to let herself believe it could be true. Not yet....

"I was an idiot," he interrupted her. "I pushed you away and it was the hardest thing I've ever done. I've regretted it every day since."

"Then...why?"

"I was scared." Nick traced a finger down the side of her face as he looked her straight in the eyes. She couldn't see anything but honesty and love shining back at her. "Jake, your family— they were everything. All I had. I mean...I had my family, but..."

"It wasn't the same," she finished for him.

"No," he agreed. "And then when I started falling for you, I was scared. I didn't want to ruin everything for something that was just a crush."

"But it wasn't just a crush." On some level, Marissa was aware the song had ended and had turned to a more upbeat party song, but they didn't move.

"No." He shook his head with a little laugh. "It was definitely not just a crush, but that night when you told me how you felt, I panicked and I did the only thing I could think of."

She dropped her gaze, but his next words made her look up again.

"It was the worst decision of my life."

"It was?"

He nodded. "Marissa, I've never stopped loving you. And obviously I'm a slow learner because I almost blew it again all because I was afraid. But you know what?"

"What?" A smile tickled the edge of her lips, because the reality of what was happening was just starting to set in.

"You *are* everything and if you feel about me even a fraction of the way I think about you, then there is absolutely nothing that should be keeping us apart."

Marissa nodded. Happiness flooded through every cell in her body. *Nick loved her.* And more than that, he stood there in front of her family and all of their friends and told her so. They weren't a secret.

"Tell me you feel the same way."

Her smile threatened to crack her face it was so wide, but Marissa didn't care. "I do," she said after a moment. "Nick, I've loved you for so long I can't remember a time when I didn't."

She had so much more she wanted to say to him, but she didn't have a chance because a moment later, his hand was behind her head, threading through her hair and pulling her close. His lips pressed to hers in a kiss that would go down as the single best kiss she'd ever had because this time as they came together, there were no questions. She wasn't left wondering about where she stood. She knew everything she needed to know.

Nick Slater loved her.

And as they kissed in the middle of the dance floor with everyone's eyes upon them, that was the only thing that mattered.

12

On some level, Nick knew maybe he should have waited to declare his love until they were alone, but he couldn't help himself because he'd already waited more than eight years. There was no way he was going to wait even one more second. It was only after he finally managed to break away from kissing Missy that he had a moment to think about what he'd just done.

Jake was going to kill him.

Nick could only hope that he waited until the end of his wedding reception. Because if Jake didn't finish the job, Jenny would.

Hoping for a quick escape outside, or somewhere else where they could avoid the questions and comments that were sure to come from friends and family, Nick took Missy's hand and led her off the dance floor. "Do you want to get out of here?" He could see in her eyes that there was nothing she would like more, but he also knew Missy. She wouldn't shirk her duties as maid of honor, no matter how much she wanted to. "Maybe just for a minute?"

She smiled, relief on her face. He would never make her

choose between her family and him. He would never again do anything that would cause her pain. "I think it would be okay if we escaped for a breath of fresh air before the cake cutting."

"Perfect." He kissed her quickly on the cheek, resisting the urge to pull her into his arms again. "I'll just go get us a quick refreshment. I'll be right back, okay, Marissa?"

She nodded, but grabbed his hand before he could leave. "One more thing." Nick couldn't help but feel a small surge of panic, but he listened anyway. "Can you call me Missy again? I kind of like it."

He burst out laughing. "Of course." And then he couldn't help himself. He pulled her close and gave her a deep kiss. "I'll call you anything you like as long as I get to call you mine."

"You sweet talker, you." She laughed and it was the sweetest sound. "Now go get me that drink."

Nick was happy to do as she requested. He moved as if he were floating. Never in his life had he felt so light and so...in love. He was so distracted as he ordered a bottle of champagne and two glasses, that he didn't notice as Jake walked up beside him until he leaned on the counter, staring directly at him.

"So," Jake said. "Is there something you need to tell me?"

The feeling of lightness vanished as Nick turned to face his best friend. Jake had always made his feelings about dating his sister very clear. *Was he about to lose the family he'd grown to love as his own?* He swallowed hard. It was a risk he was willing to take.

Besides, there was no way he could turn back now.

Nick swallowed hard, straightened his shoulders and told Jake what he should have told him eight years earlier. "I'm in love with your sister. Unbelievably, irrevocably, and completely in love with her."

Jake didn't respond and for a moment, Nick was afraid he might punch him right there in the middle of his wedding reception. Finally, he said, "I see. And how long has this been going on?"

His answer was simple. "As long as I can remember."

Jake nodded slowly. "I see...no!" He shook his head. "I don't see at all. What the hell, Nick? What's going on?"

"I love her, Jake. I always have and she loves me. I tried for so long not to feel the way I do, but it's no use and seeing her again...I won't let her get away. I'm sorry if that means you don't want to see me. I'm sorry if that ruins everything between us—I really am. But I have never felt this way about another woman, and I know I never will again. She's it for me, man. Missy is *everything*. I can't pretend anymore that I can live without her, because I can't."

Again, Jake was silent, but there was nothing else Nick could do or say. He'd laid it all out and he'd meant every word.

"Okay," Jake said after what felt to Nick like forever. "I'm not going to pretend I'm totally okay with it. I mean, not yet. It's weird and...she's my *sister*. But if you love her that much, that's all I could ever ask for for my little sister. You're a good man, Nick. The best there is. If you love her even half as much as you just said, there's no way I'm going to stand in the way of it. Besides, now you'll be my brother for real."

He couldn't help but laugh. "Don't get ahead of yourself, man." But the idea wasn't so farfetched. There was no doubt in Nick's mind that he'd slip a ring on Missy's finger the first chance he could.

Nick pulled his best friend into a man hug and slapped his back. "Thank you."

"For what?"

"For understanding." He gave Jake one more slap on the back before he pulled back. "I didn't mean to spring this on you on your wedding day, but it just couldn't wait."

"It's all good." Jake laughed.

"Can you believe it took him so long?" Alan's voice sounded behind him, and Nick turned to see the man he loved as a father there.

"What are you talking about?"

"Nick." Alan laughed. "We saw it years ago." He shook his head. "We were just waiting for you to figure it out."

He shook his head. *There was no way they had known about his feelings for Missy. And...* "What do you mean, *you all saw it*? Who are you talking about?"

"Remember when I told you I was worried there might be something going on?" Jake jumped in. "Mom tried to say something to me about it once, a long time ago, but..." Jake shook his head.

"He refused to see it," Alan said. "I think mostly, he just didn't want to see it."

"True." Jake shrugged.

"But Patrice and I saw it years ago."

Nick's head spun. "Then why didn't you say anything?"

"It had to be you, Nick," Alan said. "You had to see it."

Nick looked at Jake, who shrugged. "I guess you finally saw it." He squeezed Nick's shoulder. "Now, if you'll excuse me, I need to get back to my wife. Damn, it feels good to say that."

When he was gone, Alan shook his hand. "You have our blessing, son." He gave him a quick hug before he, too, walked away.

It took Nick a second to process everything he'd just heard before he grabbed the bottle and glasses from the bar and headed back to where he'd left Missy by the door.

It may have taken him awhile for his eyes to open completely, but now that they were, he had no intention of ever closing them. And that was a promise he fully intended to make to Missy the second he had the chance.

As much as she never wanted to be out of his arms again, it turned out to be a good thing when Nick excused himself to go get them a drink. After everything that had happened on the dance floor, she needed a minute to catch her breath.

Had he really just declared his love?

Yes.

That's exactly what he'd done. And she'd done the same and it was going to be okay.

She didn't even bother to hide her smile as she looked out over the wedding reception that she stood on the edge of. She'd never been happier in her life. And then she turned to see Nick, Jake, and her dad talking at the bar. Her heart fell for a moment but then she saw the hug and her brother's ridiculously huge smile. Relief washed through her. When her dad shook Nick's hand, she thought her heart might explode with happiness.

It would be okay.

It would be more than okay.

A moment later, her dad walked away, but not before winking in her direction, and then Nick was on his way back to her with a bottle of champagne and two glasses.

"How about we get some of that fresh air now?" he asked when he reached her.

"Absolutely." She pushed the door open and held it as he walked out into the mountain air. Marissa inhaled deeply. There was something about the mountains, or maybe it was just Castle Mountain Lodge. Whatever it was, standing outside in the slightly chilly air made her feel good. Really good.

But not as good as it felt when Nick put the drinks on a table and wrapped his arms around her again.

"How are you feeling?" He traced a finger down her cheek and tucked a stray hair behind her ear.

"Like I'm in a dream." It was absolutely the truth.

"I promise." He kissed her sweetly. "You're wide awake."

And that was the best part.

The music drifted out through the glass doors and Nick took her hand, leading her in a slow dance, despite the fast beat. When the song finished, he poured them each some champagne and raised a glass to make a toast.

Marissa raised hers as well, but when Nick didn't say anything right away, she giggled nervously. "To us?"

He shook his head. "I was going to toast to us but it seems kind of wrong not to toast to the happy couple, don't you think?"

She took a step toward him to close the distance and clinked his glass gently. "I don't think there's anything wrong to toasting to *all* the happy couples."

"Agreed."

They clinked again and both drank deeply before he once again wrapped his arm around her and prepared to kiss her again. It was as if now that they'd finally confessed their feelings he couldn't get enough of her, and that was perfectly okay with her.

Marissa closed her eyes and leaned in, prepared to lose herself in the sweet bliss that was kissing Nick, knowing he felt the same way she did.

But she didn't get that kiss. The sound of a clearing voice shattered the moment. "I don't mean to interrupt."

Marissa's eyes opened at the sound of her mother's voice. Like a teenager being caught out, she took a step away from Nick. But his hand shot out and held hers.

Her dad's lips turned up into a wry grin, but he didn't say anything. "They're getting ready to cut the cake in there and I thought you might not want to miss it."

Marissa nodded and with her free hand, smoothed down her dress. "Thanks, Mom. We'll be right in."

"I'd tell you to take your time, but..." He winked and disappeared inside.

As soon as he was gone, Marissa laughed. "Do you think she suspected anything?"

"I sure hope so." Nick pulled her hand and spun her into a quick kiss. "I'm done pretending I don't love you. I want everyone to know. I want to shout it out and I promise you right here and now, I'll never again make the mistake of not feeling each and every one of my feelings for you all the time." He kissed her again. "And, more importantly, I'll make sure you know exactly what all of those feelings are. And that's a promise."

"I believe you." And she did. With all of her heart, she believed every word he said. "Now, let's get in there before they send out a search party."

The cake cutting, like everything else Jenny had planned, was perfect. Especially the way she smashed an icing-covered piece right on her groom's nose. While the kitchen staff was preparing and slicing the rest of the cake, the DJ announced the bouquet toss. Marissa usually snuck off the dance floor and tried to hide during the traditional toss, but with Nick by her side, and her mother smiling at her across the dance floor, this time she made her way out to the dance floor with all the other single women, including Jenny's cousins, some old school friends and the requisite children.

She felt silly as the music started to play, but when she turned and saw Nick watching her carefully, those feelings vanished. She turned forward again as Jenny, her back to the crowd, raised her arms behind her head in preparation and then turned and walked directly to Marissa, where she put the bouquet in her hands before kissing her on the cheek. "It's about time," she whispered in her ear.

13

"*A*fter this, I promise your maid of honor duties will be over." Jenny handed Marissa a cup of coffee the moment she walked into the ballroom where the gift opening brunch was being set up.

Marissa took the cup greedily. She'd stayed up dancing with Nick all night and like the good best man and maid of honor that they were, they'd waited until the bride and groom had made their exit before they snuck away. It had been close to two in the morning before Marissa had finally slipped off her shoes and crawled into bed.

Alone.

Nick had been the perfect gentleman, and despite the fact that she would have loved nothing more than to spend the night wrapped in his arms, Marissa was determined to move slowly with their relationship. At least in some ways. It was too perfect, and she didn't want to spoil anything by rushing.

"How are you so perky?" she asked Jenny after her first sip of hot coffee. "I'm exhausted. You should be dead on your feet."

"No way," Jenny said. "Sleep is what honeymoons are for." She giggled. "Well...that and other things."

"Ew. You're talking about my brother." Marissa made a face, but she laughed and shook her head.

"Right." Jenny grabbed her by the shoulders and stared her in the face. "Let's talk about you and Nick."

"Oh no." Somehow Marissa managed to wiggle out of Jenny's crazy strong grip. "I don't think this is the right place. Let's talk tomorrow." She grabbed the notepad where she was supposed to write down all the gifts and made her escape.

"But we leave for Jamaica tomorrow," Jenny called after her.

That was exactly the point. Marissa smiled but her escape was short-lived when a moment later her mother grabbed her arm and steered her to the buffet line. "Good morning, sweetie."

"I'm not hungry, Mom." She was actually starving but there was no way she wanted to be cornered by her mother at that moment when guests would start arriving at any moment. It was bad enough she and Nick had shared their moment on the dance floor for everyone to see; Marissa wasn't interested in shanghaiing any more of Jake and Jenny's wedding festivities.

"You need to eat." Her mother used that tone that meant business, and Marissa knew it was pointless to try to resist. Her mother plucked the notebook from her hands and replaced it with a plate. "Even a piece of fruit. You had a late night." Her mother raised her eyebrows and Marissa was pretty sure she was going to completely combust in a humiliated flames.

"Mom!"

"Well, didn't you?"

"It wasn't nearly as late as you're insinuating. I think you raised me better than that."

Her mom laughed. "Good point."

Marissa chose a cinnamon bun with extra icing and moved along the line but her mom was right behind her. "For whatever it's worth, I think it's pretty great," she whispered into her ear.

"What?"

"You and Nick."

"I knew what you meant, Mom." She turned. "I just…"

Her mom's eyes were filled with tears. "Years ago, I thought maybe you two would…but it doesn't matter. You found each other now."

She smiled and nodded. "We did."

"And your father and I couldn't be happier."

Marissa shook her head and looked away before she, too, started crying. "Well, don't marry me off just yet, Mom. It's all still pretty new."

"Is it?"

NOTHING COULD BRING Nick down from the high he was feeling when he woke up the morning after the wedding. Not even the blinking light on his cell phone that told him he had a message.

It hadn't been hard to ignore his phone the night before. The most important people to him in the entire world were in the same room as him. But now, with Marissa already gone to the gift opening, there was no more avoiding what he had to deal with.

His father.

He'd left the suite behind and opted instead for the fresh air of the mountains to make the call he was both dreading and looking forward to. Nick didn't bother playing the message, but simply pressed the buttons that would connect him to his father.

It didn't matter that it was Sunday. His dad always worked. At the expense of everything. His relationship. His children. Everything.

The more his dad had worked, the more his mother had pulled away into some other life, that as a child he'd never understood. Now he knew she'd had a string of lovers and other interests to keep her occupied. Anything but her own family. It was one of the many reasons he'd found refuge with the Duncan family.

Despite the dysfunction of his family, it had always been understood that Nick would work for the family business one day. He'd never questioned it.

Until now.

It wasn't a decision he'd reached only the night before, although finally confessing his love to Missy definitely helped concrete how he was feeling. And besides his feelings for her, he'd never been so sure about anything in his life.

He didn't want his father's life.

The call was answered on the first ring. "Nicholas, where are you?"

His dad hardly ever used his full name.

"You know where I am, Dad. Jake Duncan got married yesterday and I—"

"That was yesterday. And I told you to be on that plane. Nick, in business, as in life, you have to make choices and—

"And I made one, Dad. I'm done."

"Pardon me?"

"I'm done. With this business. I quit."

It felt better than he'd imagined to say the words out loud.

"What?"

"I quit, Dad." It felt even better to say them for a second time.

"You can't quit."

"I just did. I don't want this."

"What's wrong with you? You don't want to be head of a multi-million dollar business company one day?"

Nick walked along the path that led around the building to the courtyard and pond where he'd kissed Missy for the scavenger hunt photo. *Had that really been two days ago?* So much had changed. *Especially the kisses.*

"No, Dad," he said. "I don't. Not if it means being like you. I want more."

His father scoffed into the phone and Nick could almost imagine him sitting behind his desk, getting more and more worked up as he realized Nick wasn't bluffing. "You want more than a power yacht in the Caribbean? A vacation house in Spain? A new sports car every few months? You want more than that?"

"I do." Nick smiled because the answer was so easy. "I want love. I want to marry the woman I love and one day have children of our own. And you know what? I want to *know* those kids. Like, really know them. I want to go to their Little League games and dance recitals. I want to give them the family they deserve instead of sending them in search of it in the family of their best friend."

On the other end of the line, his dad was quiet. For a moment, Nick wondered whether he'd gone too far. "I see," he said after a moment.

"Dad, I didn't—"

"It seems I was wrong about you." He cut him off. "You're not cut out for this job at all. I expect your resignation on my desk in the morning."

The line went dead and instead of feeling remorse, all Nick felt was relief as a weight was lifted from his shoulders. He powered his phone off and tucked it into his back pocket before heading inside.

Despite the crowd of people milling about, he saw her the moment he walked into the room. She sat next to Jenny and Jake, who were surrounded by wrapping paper and tissue. She was bent over a notepad, frantically scribbling things while Jenny opened gifts and Jake tried to look interested.

Missy radiated. She was stunning. *She was his.*

Just thinking it felt good.

"Good morning, beautiful." He made his way through the piles of paper and kissed her on the cheek, right there in front of everyone. She blushed, but turned her gorgeous eyes on him. "I was going to steal you away but you look like you have your work cut out for you here."

"You can't have her yet," Jenny said. "We have a few more."

"Seriously?" Jake groaned. "Not that I'm not grateful for everyone's generosity but I really think the tradition of the gift opening is more of a way for a bride to torture her new husband than anything else."

Nick laughed and pulled up a chair. "I'll help."

"You will?" Missy raised an eyebrow.

"If it means spending more time with you, sweetheart. Absolutely."

Jake groaned again. "It must be love."

Everyone laughed, but Nick locked eyes with Missy and with complete seriousness said, "It's most definitely love of the deepest kind. And it may not be wrapped in fancy paper and tissue," he waved his hand over the mess they were sitting in, "but, sweetheart, my love is the gift I promise to give you every day for the rest of my life."

Nick didn't care that it was cheesy. He was suddenly feeling like being very cheesy. Especially if it made Missy look at him that way. And when she leaned over and pressed her lips on his and kissed him, being cheesy was the very last thing he cared about because he'd meant every word.

THE END

If you enjoyed Promised Gifts, you'll love the next in the series, Accidental Gifts. Check out an excerpt right after a note from the author.

CASTLE MOUNTAIN LODGE

If you loved this Castle Mountain Lodge story make sure you follow up with all the characters. Below you will find links to all the books in the series, enjoy!

Unexpected Gifts - Colin & Andi's story
Hidden Gifts - Bo & Morgan's story
Unexpected Endings - Colin & Andi's short story
Secret Gifts - Gage & Megan's story
Mistaken Gifts - Jeff & Eva's story
Goodbye Gifts - Dylan & Carmen's story
Tempting Gifts - Jason & Lisa's story

Holiday Gifts - Ryan & Julie's story
Promised Gifts - Nick & Marissa's story
Accidental Gifts - Max & Tess's story

ABOUT THE AUTHOR

Elena Aitken is a USA Today Bestselling Author of more than twenty romance and women's fiction novels. Living a stone's throw from the Rocky Mountains with her teenager twins and their two cats, Elena escapes into the mountains whenever life allows. She can often be found with her toes in the lake and a glass of wine in her hand, dreaming up her next book and working on her own happily ever after.

To learn more about Elena:
www.elenaaitken.com
elena@elenaaitken.com

ACCIDENTAL GIFTS

Please enjoy an excerpt from Accidental Gifts, the next in the Castle Mountain Lodge Series

UPDATE THIS BLURB*

"Tess, you have to do it. It's not really a big deal and you'd really be helping me out."

Tess took her time swallowing the piece of muffin she'd been chewing before she answered her best friend. "No. I don't *have* to do it, it *is* a big deal and you're wrong, it would not be helping you out."

If Clara thought that in any way Tess would be helping her out by impersonating her with an important client, she was delusional. And clearly she should seek medical attention, because her delusions could be symptoms of a more serious problem.

"It really would be helping me out. This is a no-brainer job anyway."

"Thanks."

If Clara caught the sarcasm, she didn't say anything.

"I've already taken care of all the hard work. All you have to do is take the client to Mountain Ridge Outdoor Adventures and show them some of the options. It's super easy."

"He'll know I'm not you."

"No he won't," she said easily. "I've never met him. We've only chatted on the phone a few times. Mostly we've been communicating via email anyway. Please do this. You owe me."

Tess most certainly did not owe Clara anything. At least, not that she could remember. Of course, there was the time when they were seventeen when Clara took the blame for the beers her dad found in her closet. And the time when Johnny Miller broke up with her when she'd been so sure he was going to ask her to marry him instead. Clara had dropped everything and come over, spending the whole weekend eating ice cream and drinking too much wine with her.

There were lots of times like that. But surely, none of those times added up to a favor of this size.

"Clara. Even if I do owe you—" She held her finger up to silence the interruption before it began. "There is no way I can do this. You're the business consultant. Not me. I don't care how easy you *think* it is. I can't do it. I'm a payroll clerk, not a consultant. I don't know the first thing about business. I process paychecks."

"Correct me if I'm wrong." Her friend raised one eyebrow and took a sip of her drink. "But you're not processing any paychecks right now, are you? Including your own." Clara knew she had her on that point. Tess had been laid off from her job five weeks earlier and was having more than a little trouble finding a new one, which was why she'd agreed to accompany her friend to Hope Falls for a work trip in the first place. What she had most decidedly *not* agreed on was impersonating her friend while she ran off with her current boy toy to Europe on a last-minute vacation.

"You know I'm not," she grumbled and took a long sip of her latte. "You don't need to point it out all the time."

Clara pulled a folder out of her bag and slapped it on the table. "I only point it out because this is your chance to actually *earn* a paycheck."

"What?"

"You don't think I'd ask you to do this for free, do you?"

If she were honest, Tess *had* expected to do it for free. She didn't need handouts from her best friend. She wasn't totally unprepared. She had a savings account. Just like her dad had taught her when she got her first part-time job at sixteen. "Save for a rainy day, Tess. Always make sure you have at least three months' worth of your salary put away in case the unthinkable happens."

She hadn't listened to all her father's advice over the years, but she had listened to that little tidbit. Like a good girl, she dutifully saved and put away money. And she *definitely* had three months of salary put away. The only problem was, Tess took that advice when she was sixteen and working two days a week at Twisty Treat making ice cream cones. Turns out that even with ten years of interest, three months of salary from Twisty Treat a decade ago didn't add up to much. It certainly didn't add up to enough to live on for much longer than two months. If she didn't find some money, and soon, she wouldn't be able to pay rent. And she didn't even want to think about the balance on her credit card.

"How much money are we talking about?" Tess put her latte down and slowly slid the folder closer. It didn't mean she had to open it. But if it was closer...it wouldn't hurt to take a little peek...

"Normally I wouldn't do this," Clara said, "but because you'd really be helping me out with this one, I'll give you eighty percent of my fee."

"Eighty percent?" Tess would have liked to sound a lot more professional than she did, or at the very least, a little calmer. But it was hard to sound either professional *or* calm when choking on your coffee. She swallowed hard. "What type of money are we talking about?" Not that she'd turn anything down at that point, but it seemed like a logical question to ask. She flipped the folder open and scanned through the contents. "And what exactly is *Mountain Ridge Outdoor Adventures*?"

"It's this great place where they specialize in adventure activities. Just like the name suggests." Tess ignored her friend's sarcasm. "Zip-lining, horseback riding, kayaking— things like that. All you have to do is show him around and explain how he can integrate those types of activities into his existing business. I've done all the work for you. Just read my notes."

"No way." She slapped the folder shut. "Can't do it." That was putting it mildly. Tess simply did not *do* outdoor activities. Especially anything involving adventure of any kind. She was a city girl through and through. The very idea of going anywhere near a horse or a hike or anything at all that involved some sort of outdoor risk was definitely not her area of expertise. "You lost me at *outdoor.*"

"You're being ridiculous. Besides, you don't actually have to participate in any of the activities, just show him around. Meet with him a few times and go over the information I put in the file. Convince him how easy it would be and detail the pros and cons. It's all right there." Clara pointed to the file again before she flipped through a few pages to a contract. "Including my fee," she added. "Remember. You'll get eighty percent."

Tess's eyes trailed down the page to where her friend was pointing and immediately widened. "Eighty percent? You're sure?"

Clara nodded.

Tess swallowed hard. *Decision made.* She was pretty sure she could put up with some dirt and a few bugs if it meant paying her rent for the next few months and maybe even taking care of some of that pesky credit card balance.

"So, you're in? Because I think I saw his car pull up."

"What?" Tess managed to pull her gaze away from the contract long enough to glare at her best friend. "Now?"

Clara's smile was sweet. "Yes. Remember, you're Clara Clark. Everything you need to know is in here and the client's name is Maxwell Grant. Here he comes."

With one final death stare at Clara, Tess turned around in her chair just in time to watch the sexiest man she'd ever laid eyes on walk through the door.

It had already been a long day. After a flight to Lake Tahoe, followed by a forty-five minute drive to the town of Hope Falls, the last thing Max wanted to do was have a meeting inside. He'd much rather tie his hiking boots on and hit the trails. For the last few hours, the scenery of the Northern California mountains had been tempting him and he was itching to get outside and explore.

It had been less than twenty-four hours since he'd been at Castle Mountain Lodge, surrounded by the Canadian Rockies. From what he'd seen, Hope Falls was a very quaint little town, but he missed being outdoors. With any luck, the initial meeting with the consultant wouldn't take terribly long and he could go exploring.

There weren't many people in the little coffee shop, and his eyes immediately locked on a table with two women. Two very beautiful women. Maybe he could tolerate being inside for a little while longer. The blonde smiled broadly in his direction. She had to be Clara Clark.

"Hi there." He extended his hand. "You must be—"

"I'm Tess," she interrupted. "This is Clara. You must be Maxwell Grant, her client."

"Max." He tilted his head and looked at the brunette, who still sat quietly. She seemed to undergo some sort of transformation while he watched and must have remembered why she was there. Her pretty mouth turned up into a smile that didn't quite reach her eyes and she stood.

"Sorry about that," she said. "I'm usually a little more prepared." She glanced quickly at her friend. "Why don't we all get some fresh coffee and get to know each other?"

"Oh no," Tess said. "I have to get going and the two of you probably have a lot of work to do. I wouldn't want to get in the way. Besides, I have a flight to catch."

"That's too—"

"I think you have time," Clara interrupted him and focused on her friend. "Your flight doesn't leave for a while yet and there's always time to have a coffee." She gritted her teeth and gestured with her head to the table.

"Oh, I would if I could." The blonde stood from the table and gathered her purse. "But I'm sure you both have important work to do. So I'll go. Besides, there's a car waiting for me outside." She blew them both a kiss.

"A car?"

Max took a step back and watched the exchange between the two friends with a shake of a head. He might be an expert outdoorsman who'd come a little too close to a grizzly once or twice, scaled sheer rock faces, and rafted some of the worlds wildest rapids, but women were one thing he didn't think he'd ever get a handle on.

"Must run, darlin'. I'll touch base with you later this week."

And just like that, the bubbly blonde was gone and Clara looked stricken.

"Are you okay?" Max pulled a chair over and guided her to sit down again. "You look a little pale. Let me get you some water."

"Oh no. I'm—" She put her hand on his arm and the touch immediately sent a shock through him. Her too, obviously, as she stumbled over her next words. "I'm okay. I mean...I'm fine. I was just...never mind." She yanked her hand away and opened the file. "We should probably get to work."

Work was the last thing on Max's mind, especially after that touch. But it was the responsible thing to do. After all, the management of Castle Mountain Lodge had hired him to do a job and they were footing the bill for his trip to Hope Falls in an effort for him to collect as much information as he could about opening up an adventure park. For an outdoorsman like him, it was the perfect job. And he wasn't going to screw it up.

"I think that's a good idea, Clara." He pulled out a chair and sat across from her, trying not to focus on how pretty she was and how she didn't look anything at all like he'd pictured. She was softer somehow than the ambitious, no-nonsense tone of her emails. But then again, a lot could get lost in translation through email. Including the chemistry that obviously sizzled between them.

Read the rest of Accidental Gifts now!